MAKENZY ORCEL

The Emperor

TRANSLATED BY NATHAN H. DIZE

LONDON NEW YORK CALCUTTA

The work is published with the support of the
Publication Assistance Programmes of the Institut français

Seagull Books, 2024

Originally published in French as *L'Empereur*
© 2021, Editions Payot & Rivages

First published in English translation by Seagull Books, 2024
English translation © Nathan H. Dize, 2024

ISBN 978 1 80309 366 6

British Library Cataloguing-in-Publication Data
A catalogue record for this book is available from the British Library

Typeset by Seagull Books, Calcutta, India
Printed and bound in the USA by Integrated Books International

To Nyl

Ain't got no God

—Nina Simone

I haven't stopped leaving, cursing myself . . .

THE TOTALITY OF ABSENCE

Somewhere in the countryside, in an enclosure the size of about three plots of land, a shepherd reigns supreme over a flock of sheep, almost completely unaware of who they really are, from their true names to the contours of their faces. They bleat, idolize and venerate their master's glass ceiling to please Earth and the gods.

The Emperor-Shepherd, which is to say, the one who knows, ordains, completes, punishes, forgives and reigns from his armchair, seated in the shade of the baobab tree or on the terrace of the Patriarch's house adjacent to the badji, the ounfò, the sacred temple. The most beautiful house in all the lakou, with its numerous rooms furnished like they were in the past. In the smallest room is a banquet composed of all sorts of meats, vegetables, grains and alcoholic beverages offered to the gods, just in case the gods feel a little peckish at any time of the day or night.

This house is also the office of the kay mistè, the place where the Emperor-Shepherd initiates contact with those who have disappeared, through the medium of an interstellar jar, the govi. Creating a pandemonium of which he is the one and only arbiter, he hides behind a white sheet symbolizing the purity of his soul, shielding him from the gaze of those outside. During this operation, no one has the right to speak the intercessor's name at the risk of plunging him further into the beyond to be stuck there, forever. But in reality, the whole thing is rigged. The Emperor-Shepherd is pretending. It's a jar like any other. There is no tool for communicating with the gods and the deceased, no transcendence, no interpretation, nothing paranormal at work. He's still the one who speaks, loves and punishes, the one who plays the role of the emancipated gwobonzanj who must subsequently return to the continent from which his African forefathers had been separated. Among other deceitful operations, he's an impostor. He's taking everyone for a ride.

The other houses planted around the Emperor's are not homes, but narrow sheep pens, ajoupas, huts, used to corral an entire flock of absent souls, followers who are force-fed truths and falsehoods by the mystical master for the good of their souls. All it takes is for one of them to go astray, to baa and for this bleating to fall out of sync, voluntarily or involuntarily, with the preestablished and accepted melody, causing them to fall before the hands of the Sacred. It's forbidden for them to no longer obey; the head of one faces the ass of another, all together behind the Emperor.

Even so, there is no barbed-wire fence surrounding this part of Earth, no armed guard to prevent these animals from escaping. They're bound by sanctified chains, rendered blind and mute by their ignorance, their excessive faith in this god on Earth whose word is the most powerful of drugs. What kind of absolute and astonishing truth might be necessary to draw the sheep out from here?

Years later, after having been plunged into this silence for too long, a voice emerges. Conscious, discordant and trenchant—his words are a blaze in the dark of the night. Nothing more than memories pulling at his tongue.

ONE

Knock knock knock!

It's not the police. Not yet. Someone must have the wrong door. But I know that they'll be here in one moment or the next, in uniform, armed with their frustration. An entire procession. Just for me. A lone, unarmed man. They should be here already. They won't have any difficulty connecting me to what happened. In addition to their heavy artillery, they'll be armed to the teeth with their end-of-the-month difficulties, their pitiful working conditions, their fears, their doubts for the future. I won't stand a chance. The horde of officers will kick the door in and won't even think twice about it. They don't knock on doors here. What I've done, as cruel as one might think it was—I had to do. I have no regrets. I even held on to the evidence. It's there. Right next to me. The suit carefully folded. The briefcase, etc. I came home. I got undressed. I put my normal clothes back on. Then, with slow and methodical gestures, I folded my suit. The vial in the inside pocket of the coat made me jump with unspeakable joy. When I felt it between my fingers, knowing what it was capable of in just a few seconds—the miraculous hope it contained. I replay the final expressions the bastard made. He got what he deserved. When I think about the dexterity and the success with which I executed my plan, aided by the sorcerous voice inside myself that I call 'the Other Within', I have to acknowledge him. In my childhood he whispered things to me. Opened my eyes to the world around me. And each time, it was as though he awakened me from a deep slumber. More than just a voice, he's a dark and fragile creature whom I love and cannot resist.

When we feel trapped, under siege in the deepest part of ourselves, when we cannot see things otherwise—we could always do worse . . . The stories that emerge from prison are chilling and terrifying. It's hardly the appropriate place from which to address someone in complete freedom. In prison, you have to fight for every breath. The inmates are piled in like in the belly of a slave ship, the cells saturated with disease, the stench of shit and resignation. One hundred detainees in a space meant for twelve. The guards torture them to relieve themselves of boredom. It's the longest, most odious march towards death. The detainees are death itself. When you no longer have any hope or last resorts, you might as well admit you're dead . . . But even prison and its horrors cannot force me to feel remorse. Let them lock me up, isolate me from society, punish me, allow me to atone for the freedom to love, for trusting my instincts to the very end.

TWO

It feels so good to have nothing left to lose, nothing at all. I recognized the weight I was carrying. This suit and everything else, it's not just the tangible, irrefutable proof of my guilt, but proof that nothing will ever be the same.

If only we could liberate ourselves from the past . . . And begin again.

Oh, sinner, where will you run?

I asked for none of this. I was waiting for the bus. I was waiting for forever. I think I've been waiting since I was born. I sat on the floor for hours, fighting the urge to sleep. Looking beyond the clouds of dust that covered the horizon. The days went by, one looking just like the other. The bus wouldn't come. There's too much countryside to travel, too many children to collect along these deserted roads, each of them sculpted from fear, hunger and a voracious desire to live. Their faces closed, spoilt like tragic fruit. This world devours the innocent. Before they die, there are some who lose the ability to speak. All they succeed in saying is *shit*. A word that they've trudged through their whole lives. I must have been thinking about the lucky star beneath which you had to have been born to leave this cursed place when, all of a sudden, a shadow grabbed hold of me. You picked me up like something you had left behind only to pick back up later. You took me there, to the lakou. You taught me how to play the drums—rather, you stuck a drum between my legs. And there I was, a restavèk, a slave, a sheep, an entertainer for the spirits, tasked with calling upon them. Without asking yourself if it suited me to live in a lakou, to initiate contact with the ancestors in Ginen, the spiritual epicentre, the land of our great roots, of which our country is an offshoot, the heir.

I just wanted to get onto the bus. To leave. To no longer be a link in your long chain of successful lies. A brick in your wall. Otherwise, I would've never ended up here in this place that I've paid for with the money I've earned by the sweat of my brow. I would've never been free. And free I will be once more, even after the police arrive to beat me down, walk all over me, crush me and all the other things we allow only criminals to endure, before putting me in handcuffs and tossing me in their wagon on a one-way trip to hell. It feels unavoidable.

THREE

What was I doing on the side of the road? Unfortunately, it's a story I'll never be able to tell, because I don't know what happened. Certain accounts suggest that after a hurricane ravaged the southern region of the country, surviving families, desperate and powerless, gave their children up to nature. I must have been one of these children, abandoned there for whoever wanted me. I have a vague memory of a hand caressing my cheeks, of a soft and broken voice that told me, 'Wait right there, sooner or later the bus will appear; get on board and let the bus take you far away. Never forget that your parents have, and always will, love you.' Sometimes I still look at the world with the same greed and intensity with which I stared down that lost and desolate road.

I've never stopped leaving, cursing myself . . .

I know I'm free.

You must've had to convince yourself that it was a disease, an evil spell, due to my reluctance to serve the gods the way they deserved. What god, what master can imagine what a sheep or a slave ponders as they lie down in the straw at night? The depth of their anger is born of this feeling of nothingness.

Sometimes, you have to go looking for ammunition in silence. I admit that it took me some time to break the silence. To drown you out. To put a name to the chasms inside you that even the gods, by failing to make you one of their children, a true initiate, didn't know how to exorcize ...

Just as a man's dignity doesn't come to an end at nightfall, you cannot remedy the past. I'll continue to express my deepest thoughts, the way I've done for some time by hacking out the bitterness that has built up in the back of my throat for too long. So that I can finally breathe, rather than hope for repentance for the kind of Emperor you were. I've made my words an outlet in this world that brings death to freedom. Don't be surprised that I leant into life's turns the way I did before being interrupted by the *knock knock knock* on the door. To me, it was nothing more than a vast, sinister tale. Life in the lakou. The mystical omnipresence you claimed to represent, that you exuded like the smoke from your pipe. It's been on my mind for years, sometimes to the point of self-blame; it's time my silence stops following me around like a string of bad luck. As prisoners of our own truths, we've seen ourselves on the other side of a mirror before, in a place where time seems to have been crafted by the shape of our dreams, and when they crumble, our eyes open to the ineptitude of the world, leaving us with the horrible feeling that we no longer exist, or perhaps only in part ...

FOUR

For the Other Within, life is a monologue. A path we follow on our own. The other we encounter is nothing more than a brief improvisation, a detour towards possibility, a turn inward . . .

I often talk to my shadow or to myself. I'm not sure when or how it started. Sometimes these conversations carry on for a while before I realize that I'm also scratching myself and it burns. Before I can tear my hands away from my body, this fluvial mirror. There comes a moment of nothingness, and yet, I do not lose touch with reality.

We must place our trust in others, they can help us take possession of ourselves, I don't remember who told me this. I wasn't entirely convinced. Other people are also solitary, dry, lacking a sense of self . . .

Right in the middle of a ceremony, during an ordinary trance, I could swim deep into my thoughts, lifting my feet off the ground so that the spirits could not trace the path taken by my senses. I imagined, for example, one of your fictional characters, an infantile god living in an immense glass house deep in outer space. My intergalactic buddies and I would ride through the halls of time on bicycles, travelling for light years, through different perspectives of infinity, electric and gravitational forces, and all their associated properties. We played in parallel universes, the sun, the moon, the Earth within our grasp. We crafted planets with the fragments of fallen stars that would remain unknown to the likes of man. We explored the origins of everything and every living being. We encountered other veiled hierarchies, digging deeper into new depths . . .

I'm not sure you can comprehend these distances or, for that matter, the meaning of these imaginative acts, because for you, love, integrity and every unimportant thing was nothing more than the blowing wind, a price to pay, nothing to write home about. Your manoeuvres, your lies were sufficient. Oh, your famous lies! How you loved crafting them. You were nothing without them, the most precious things you possessed, as intimate as our hopes of the afterlife we whisper into animals' ears right before cutting off their heads. The gods are watching us, listening at our doors, to our heartbeats, reading the curvature of our slightest thoughts, loving one another so the day may break, syncopating the rhythms of the heart, breathing through every glance, every glimmer of the day, every appearance of the moon, every man's hand at work, in the laughter of children, aware of the day each of us will die, and their names protect us from evil, from our fatal attractions, drunk off the sea and the oceans. The air we breathe is nothing more than the breath of Dambala or Ayida; the Black Empyrean is reserved for the unwavering, the obedient. This bullshit, as it were, coursed through your veins, some of it more abracadabraesque than the rest. You were good at finding this nonsense, making it crackle in the air. It filled your mouth—you—the Emperor who was supposedly our guide. Your lies were an impenetrable fog, your true victory.

FIVE

I see you again through this sad, repugnant past, like the open wound that is this city. You are tall, skinny, your shoulders oscillate, your back is slightly curved, your beard thick and grey, concealing the better part of your stony face, your eyes are wrinkled like a crocodile's and your gait is simple, deliberate. My nostrils still tickle from your usual pungent scent—freshly cut grass. It plunges me into a sea of memories I would like to forget, to erase. You must be so old now, struggling to hide your trembling hands, retrenched in your solitude, your gaze empty, awaiting death, or perhaps dead for some time. The temple disgraced. The lakou, a hazy landscape, deserted by the spirits. Whatever the case, your years as Emperor are no longer ahead of you. Allow me to disturb your slumber by lending my voice to the dust, to the rivers, to the plants, to the birds, to the centre tree, to the drum, to the Very Old Sheep . . .

You were always the only one to speak, the great, pensive master at the centre of attention, at once the shepherd and the top dog, there, where time begins and the horizon ends. What should have been a cause for concern provoked an immense sense of pleasure. Enclosing living beings and things behind the barricade of your egocentrism. Enslaving them with your false truths . . .

You knew how to addle the minds of these moronic sheep, how to crush them, how to impose trances and oh so many chimeras upon them. Diverting their gaze from reality. Sowing within them the vanity of hope. Gallivanting the deceased before their eyes. The lwa and their adventures, perched on a tiny branch at the apex of a tree, or this nèg-triton taming the oceans . . . Under the guise of a family, you created the state. An inegalitarian regime. Slavery. Your children were not children. Your women were neither empresses, nor queens, nor manman dlo, but margins creased before your pre-eminence, sacrificed for the glory of the shepherd. Despite your vicious motivations—the glaring inequalities intensified since your inauguration, melding this sense of fear with a bitterness provoked by your presence— the sheep were incapable of imagining a future for themselves. The very thought was unbearable to them, living in a world without a leader where everyone has the same amount of time to speak, the same amount of humanity, the same amount of food on their plate and water in their cup. A lakou without an Emperor, without gods to serve, is nothing more than a patch of directionless, soulless earth. Nothing belongs to the sheep. Everything belongs to the Invisibles, the names you evoked to wrest everything from them. You would order the mountains to drown themselves in the sea if they questioned your splendour. The first sheep that left the pen without your authorization—

the one who expressed its discontent—was soon punished, banished, cursed. Even the child that was stillborn—we cut its umbilical cord with a shard of a broken bottle or a rusty blade before planting it beneath the baobab, so that the branches would continue to grow with the child in the afterlife and trace a path to our African ancestors—we were not allowed to grieve. Since their life was cut short by the will of the gods, they were like a passing sunset. Others occur with greater clarity and a warmer welcome. Africa was a trance into which I could never enter. A promised land, so close, and yet lost, disoriented, maternal, forbidden. We were forced to lower our gaze and admire the gods. Self-effacement and crushing shame were signs of respect, of submission.

SIX

Only the Emperor is granted the power of the word. To mould them to the shape of his heart, his anger or his madness. What words capable of cauterizing wounds are not also accused of being lost or eternal? Yours were difficult to grasp. They reminded us of fond memories of the gods. Their goal was to intercede in our favour. To save us. To destroy us. To bring truth, morality and the past to an end. To transform others into obedient machines. A widespread and lucrative venture. You made a fortune off the penniless and their spoilt crumbs, their ill-gotten gains. You recreated an ancient formula.

And your words—a detour leading to even more innuendos and shadows—struck at the heart of nothing. Your words floated in mid-air. I wondered when they would decide to land, blending with reality. You exhausted yourself to make certain they were overblown, saying more than you wished them to. The wind blows, confiding in us its flame. We can feel it. It'll blow again tomorrow. Contrary to each word you pronounce and each breath you draw, it's neither a sketch nor a troubled dream. You needed to know once and for all that we were not all livestock. You must have felt it, seen it swelling in my evasive stare (which didn't flee your own, but surveyed the route, seeking the bus from my childhood), I was the disruptive element, the virus, the one sceptical of all forms of doctrine, the imperfect sheep, the one who does not wait to be invited, to be told to go ahead and graze. Otherwise, you would not have chased me away, because your self-importance and your power feed off the sluggishness of the submissive, the resigned, the spineless, the cowards who never dare to defy you, addicted as they are to the torments you inflict upon them. You couldn't believe you were hearing the found child launching into a sarcastic questioning of an authority figure, a long patriarchal tradition, a system, a despot, your livelihood. Ha ha ha, I imagine you as though struck by lightning! Like a cat fallen into a boiling cauldron. Blessed be Bawon Samdi! The little ingrate, how could he?! I adopted him, made him into a man . . .

I'm not speaking to the Emperor. There's no longer an Emperor that holds. If there were, the student, the disciple, the little lamb would have to no longer be free of the fate you traced for him. I'm just a man looking another man, you, in the eyes, telling him everything. I know, it's unheard of. Nobody has ever spoken about you, or any other Emperor, this way before. In the lakou, such an act would be unimaginable. To do away with truth, confines, the rules, the secrets, the injustices. Especially to free oneself from your professorial voice, infused with more knowledge about life and death than everyone else.

SEVEN

What Emperor can stare beyond his nose into the abyss that his govi places before him? What mystical, historical inheritance could have originated with you? You lied about life, death, the afterlife, your oracular aura. About your parents being black angels floating off to heaven, alive, in an azure whirlwind. And what else? Every day, with an uncanny resolve, you wove even more threads into your stories. Waging war against the dread that we might discover the fool cloaked in the robes of the Sacred. But sometimes the tongues, drunk as they can be after a ceremony, loosened and risked it in the forbidden reaches of the formidable swamps. All the versions lined up. For example, your parents never floated off to heaven. They served in this lakou for years, in humble and devoted service to the lwa until the evening when, after a prolonged agony, they rendered their souls to the afterlife. So that they would not depart without your blessings, they sent for their eldest son. But he was nowhere to be found . . .

If life had wished for me to know my parents, to be something other than an abandoned child, I don't see why I wouldn't have been proud. You don't let your parents die in solitude or shame, deprived of the final funerary dance.

And yet, the eldest son was there, somewhere.

It was all planned, you had to escape from this hell. This fucking country where Providence remained beyond everyone's dreams. You left full of youth, searching for something better in the city. A few moons were all it took for oblivion to get the better of you, clouding the contours of your face. You became a distant memory, erased, a subject hardly ever mentioned. And, all of a sudden, as though by magic, you emerged from the abyss and paraded around the deserted landscape of the lakou, swimming in your overalls, sporting a straw hat, a red handkerchief, a pipe, a basket made from latania leaves, multicoloured bobbles and a machete, just like Kouzen Zaka, the protector of the fields and livestock. I see you like a fantastical jester whose steps are measured by the millimetre, flung far and wide, to the end of eternity, so these hicks recognize what sets you apart—your superiority. All you needed to do was pass through the lakou. Life is an interminable charade. But never before had you been so prodigious. Nevertheless, the climate was entirely in your favour. Desperation thrived in the countryside. Nobody could remember seeing you talk to anyone. Showering the earth with kleren. Or drawing a piece of bread from your basket to place it in the mouth of a lwa or a little brat. It was midday. The wild sun was drumming the earth with its millions of terrible arms. One of your future wives, seated at the foot of the baobab, her face buried in one of her hands, her eyes fixed on the plains, seemingly in search of freedom. In noticing you, she lifted her gaze, illuminating her disillusioned features, and thought—only a lwa could possess such elegance and stature. And at this exact moment, you were the deliverance, the elixir, the sustenance, the peace she was waiting for. This thought must have weighed on her spirit like the clearest of evidence, and its materialization was indispensable, vital for her and everyone else. An absolute necessity. A dream to be realized at whatever the cost. You continued to walk. As the afternoon dwindled, shadows crowded around the baobab, the plains in the background, your silhouette circled by a vortex of dust, as though everything had been planned to make the scene even more dramatic, even more supernatural. The girl (who you bled in your canopy bed every night since your consecration) still dreamt of the future without taking her eyes off you . . .

None of the people gathered there that day, around your parents' bodies, had any idea that the eldest son we'd sent for was about to become the self-appointed Emperor. That the Patriarch they were waiting for had just entered the enclosure, beautiful and crowned in an unfamiliar splendour.

It was late at night. The corpses started to cool. Expanding. Spreading a foul odour that clings on to you. The customs of the lakou dictated that those close to the departed would look upon them one final time and wish them safe passage. Beneath the benevolent clarity of the moon, folks glanced once more, their noses buried in handkerchiefs, hoping to see you again, that you would come back to fulfil your duty as a son. But you showed up again one week later, after the burial, wearing the same clothing, sent by the gods watching over this spiritually deprived lakou. You were their Emperor, their saviour. Everyone was unanimous, blinded by a thirst to be led, to be dominated. It was the beginning of your glory. Of course, you weren't there for no reason.

'Who am I,' you maintained, 'to carry out such a mission? I've long dreamt of the life of a traveller, a wanderer. I prepared myself for a life on the road, but who can escape the good graces of the gods, to question the clarity of their vision, to live without their knowledge? They called upon me, so I came . . .'

Your voice was convincing, as clear as that of an elected official, a conscript, the purest of all horsemen. Ewes, rams and lambs listened to you religiously, seated on the ground, admiring, forgetting your parents' episode and the shame in which they departed. They listened to you, not wanting to know a thing about you, as though it were written, you were granted this land as an appanage, you were a new creature, all olden things were bygone, and now everyone had to listen to you, nay, listen to the gods through you. And once your knowledge was recognized by these halfwits, the rest was just a formality. Nothing, nobody could stop you from becoming Emperor, the living passage between the gods and the rest of us mere mortals. Religious exaggeration possesses no equal in any other realm of life. You made sure that you were praised and courted. There was a whole month during which your hands were insufficient to receive all the presents, food, money, attractive girls and oaths of loyalty. It took on the allure of patronal feasts, munificent jubilations, for nothing more than to loosen your foreign tongue, to mark the moment of first contact. All the resources wasted thanks to a pretender, thanks to a debauched god who had fallen, twisting its ankle—ay!

EIGHT

Of all the lost sheep in the lakou, one revealed his scepticism towards these changes, as evil as they were absurd. As such, was he the only one who understood what had previously terrified the lakou? Was he the only one who comprehended what he and the others had fought against to establish a new way of life and that it was to the point of reappearing in the form of something even more savage? He was known as the Very Old Sheep. And he saw it coming. He spoke to me, but he couldn't see me. He had lost his vision. His life, too. It's the same thing. A huge burn mark on his face. It was frightening because you would've thought that this part of his face had come unglued, like it was ready to fall off at any moment. Seated, or rather, lost, in a chair whose worn-out straw revealed his scarified buttocks, he rotted admirably in the sunshine. I don't know what happened to him. He only told me a little piece of it later on. But his story wasn't so different from everyone else's.

Instead of being like you, a crook disguised as a shepherd, the Very Old Sheep had resigned himself to being what he would be until his death, a waste of wisdom, a mapou defrocked of all its leaves. All that he had left were his words, trenchant and essential, to be used with the discretion of his meditative, nearly silent voice. From time to time, we spent long hours watching the dust pirouette in the sky. I mean, shit! How can I describe it? I often imagined a wall of wings traversing the sky, I am part of the immense flock. I hold onto the memory of an honest and profoundly altruistic man. I listen to him attentively every time I have the chance.

In the beginning, I didn't understand why, before he started talking, he always asked me where he, the overseer, was. You were the overseer. What happened between the two of you for him to be so afraid of opening his mouth in your presence? There was reason to wonder. He wouldn't wait long to tell me everything. 'The coast is clear,' I told him. Without delay, he started to whisper.

Despite his old age, his diminished faculties, a candle away from his final breath, the Very Old Sheep's voice didn't waver. His voice had maintained its vehemence and richness. Throughout his childhood, he had been a sturdy and attentive boy in the wise shadow of the Elders who took it upon their hearts to administer the lakou. To ensure the unity of the family and to prepare it spiritually and militarily in case of the eventual return of the Western colonizers whom the African Spirits had aided us in purging from this Haitian soil. He was Bokonon, the consultant and interpreter of the fa, which was, according to him, the source of dreams, containing the answers to all the questions posed by humanity. The guiding light that makes it possible to

follow a life across time, even after its disappearance . . . To serve
what is just, that was our motto, he continued, smiling through
his eclipsed, nostalgic eyes. Vodou linked us to history, to the real
and distant elements present in the Universe. Vodou offered us
deliverance, so that we could become more firmly rooted. The
Very Old Sheep dedicated his body and soul to it, and also
regretted certain deviations which are sometimes, in his opinion,
indispensable to understanding and continuing to grow. There
was also an allusion to a woman. A woman never tells stories, my
son. You must love her, it's that simple. He loved her more than
all the lwa in the pantheon. She came from afar, from New
Orleans, or Savannah, in search of truth. One of humanity's
truths that she had found, located in a single man, like a warm
and constant light in the heart of the world's madness. Far from
the preserved, prefabricated 'voodoo' on display in America. Far
from the gadgets. The 'voodoo' dolls. The purple parades in your
Sunday best. Spirituality in all its forms. He had never seen such
a beauty. In her voice, the Vodou songs reached peaks far beyond
the ethereal world of the govi. She danced the bamboula, the ibo,
the nago. And dancing along with her was the lakou, the denuded
mountains, the baobab, the sheep. Her love of dance and life were
adorable. Sometimes she would disappear for six months, a year
even, without sending news. That's just how she was.

It didn't bother me. Our love, like our words, need a chance
to breathe. To inhabit many possibilities simultaneously. It's
foolish to limit yourself to the same story, or to always tell it in

the same way, from the beginning. When she returned, it was our first time all over again, our first kiss, our first everything. Still just as intense, magical, and my God, the stories she told about her wanderings, we sometimes laughed until we couldn't breathe. A man pretended to have seen the Pharoah's reflection in the Nile. In Salvador de Bahia, a woman drowned in her herbal bath. One evening, in a village in Benin, she had witnessed a charlatan lower the moon onto a black enamelware plate and then call the children to come see and remember this miracle. They were all astonished, except the one who cried, 'That's not the moon, but its shadow . . .' The Very Old Sheep had narrated other equally fascinating things to me, but he never could recall the rest of his wife's journey.

NINE

You had chosen our fate. We were black sheep destined to be sacrificed in a holocaust. Mistakes of nature. Except for one who was special. A pudgy, intense kid with a crazy face who scratched his ass right in your face. Defiled your cultish objects. Blasphemed. Cursed. Spit. As though the entire world was responsible for the fact that he was right there, in this small, backward place with this old devil. Withstanding your gaze by opening his mouth to spew nonsense. It was his word against yours. The great spiritual leader rejected by a child in the presence of his sheep. I had never seen anything so inexcusable. Shocked, I remember turning discreetly in your direction to study your reaction, the expression on your face. You didn't look like you took it seriously at all. As though he hadn't just disrespected you and all the sacred things you were supposed to defend and teach others to respect.

These scenes recurred for many long, heavy days. And we little sheep also continued, on the other hand, to suffer the foul temper and nastiness of this boy. 'Why are you so dirty? Go wash yourselves! Scrub good and hard! Then hurry back so I can get a lick in. I also want you to bring me back some burning firewood with your bare hands, jumping like a hot potato!' He was the kind of creature you snuff out when the right moment presents itself. Even the Very Old Sheep, the nicest man, the most inoffensive man I've ever known, would have applauded this idea. I couldn't stand him either. Rightly treated him like the crooked wood. But when it came to disciplining the little shit, I could only dream of it. I would lay him out on the ground and kick him until his body ceased to move, annihilated. I would wake up fearing the crime I had just committed might become reality, because the gods are with us when we sleep—another one of your lies. I realized the extent to which you were a hypocrite, silent when it was convenient for you. Indifference was nothing more than another form of impotence imposed by a force greater than your infinite spirits. And animals of your kind, driven by a desire for omnipresence, often forget that the well of lies isn't bottomless.

Time blossoms, flourishes and withers, lamentably. The wind drags debris behind the dust, like the vulture takes off with its prey. Then, just like the new year, before beginning the preparations for the festival of the gods, out of nowhere, the kid approached everyone, one after the other, 'Goodbye friends, it's been a pleasure knowing you,' under the satisfied gaze of his father who had just climbed down from his vehicle, walked towards the shadow of the baobab and handed you an envelope of money. I imagined the kid was either a criminal on the run that they'd hidden in the lakou for a certain sum of money, waiting for the case to die down. The police and the judicial system are scared to death of Vodou and its Mysteries, for nothing in the world would they want to have anything to do with them—sometimes, just like their victims, they have no other option than to turn to the supernatural. Or he was there for a ritual service, a magical treatment, an herbal bath administered by the oungan, the seer that you were not. To purge from his mind the voices and whims of unknown and malevolent nations. To save his son, the man was prepared to do anything. He had consulted many medical specialists in vain. While he cried in the hallway of the hospital, a nurse approached him, looked him directly in the eye and said, 'Monsieur, if I were you, I would put my feet into water.' In other words, the malady that ails your son cannot be healed by a doctor. This world cannot do a single thing for you. You need a doktè fèy. A perfect traditional healer. An Oungan-Ginen, a seer with spirits who travel through his mind ... You, an interloping horse, had assessed the situation. If there was nothing you could do, everything was fucked.

Never had a situation been so alarming as to earn your compassion. On the contrary, it was a chance to stuff your pockets even more. The gods, the greedy ventriloquists from whom you learnt your avarice and your bad faith, doubled, tripled, quadrupled the cost of your intervention. They arrived all the way from Africa. They had to eat and drink. All of that was very costly. Often, a man, a woman, or a family would ask to see the spiritual leader. You invited them behind your white sheet. After a moment, they re-emerged with a sense of relief on their faces, prostrating themselves, as though all of it were true. Under no circumstances could anyone doubt your extra-lucidity, your talents as an enchanter, a teller of wild adventures.

You swindled even the most incompetent who indebted themselves or brought you their valuables to settle a bill for a treatment that wasn't one. After a few of your phony hypnotist antics—including, among others, a mixture of random leaves, a tarot-card reading, followed by a leap back in time through the govi calling on multiple escorts for the sacrifice of a pig—you claimed that the moon would take a little time in showing its true face, that the gods had many cases to consider, but that they still possessed the goodness to place the child at the top of their list of priorities. It cannot wait. Then you spun around the baobab seven times and had a vision. The soul of the young boy had been ripped from the forces of darkness. Now, he was free. He climbed into his father's car. Some good business for you, an end to the hostility for the rest of us insignificant little things.

I never forgot. Everything is there. All I have to do is close my eyes.

TEN

Then came the time to get rid of me. This time, the bus came. The other children must have been swallowed by the dust and oblivion . . . my forehead had already been marked by the iron seal of life. Rebellious spirits. Insolent children. Hardheads. They're punished. They're kicked out of the house of the gods in whom their fate was trusted. They're thrown into the face of the world. You didn't flinch. Better to die than to see someone approach the boundaries of your laws. I shouldn't have sought answers to my questions, to fill in my voids. I should have let them swallow me whole. To be an exemplary sheep, fall in line. But I slipped voluntarily, I cursed myself, never mind you. And my hubris would lead me to my doom.

You weren't chasing away a member of the family by getting rid of me for my flagrant disobedience. You expelled a parasite. A mistake that no longer had its place in history. An Emperor gathers, tosses out and takes back as he pleases. Nobody could challenge what was before your eyes. You acted in the name of the Sacred, the afterlife, the inexplicable, in the name of that which exceeded our understanding. Build a house and furnish it, only to set it ablaze afterwards, that must be how the gods entertain themselves through the day.

The ruminant song goes, *manman m ki fè m, m sòti nan trip li, gade m manje l*—my mother, who gave me life, carried me in her guts and watches me consume them, hasn't escaped my tyrannical laws.

I'm not coming back to weep, to divert you from your path, nor to undergo the trials of the earth and the spirits. The earth is the mother, the wife, the sister, the sensitive girls beaten, raped, murdered. The gods are fashioned of bits by despair.

I'm not coming back to weep. I'm trying to emerge from the absence. The world didn't break me. You prepared me, reluctantly, for its tyranny, its inhumanity. The shock was violent. But, little by little, a man's life is forged at the margins of this urban abyss into which so many others dive, losing themselves forever. Torrents of falls that look like nothing. They follow every day, one after the other, always in the same order, more and more deafening and forgettable. The scent of failure crowds my nostrils. I force myself to hold my head above the tide. As many times as the waves rose, as many times my eyes triumphed over tears. I followed detours, opened holes, built internal cities. I distanced myself as far as possible from death.

I still feel the anxiety, the imbalance triggered by the unknown, the unexpected, the terrifying spectre of the future, but I know how to cope with it better now. I pursue life, tame it and open to it the darkest reaches of myself. My latent existence, I murdered the zonbi that you wanted me to become. The picked-up child, the sheep, the restavèk—he's dead. He no longer carries the name you gave him, like all those who came into this world under your reign. An alphanumerical composite referring to my date of birth or a lwa's favourite number, I can't remember any more. But I should remember. You cannot forget your name. But it wasn't a name. I wasn't a person, the son of an adopted nation. I was a product, a detainee, a code, a head of livestock, an indentured servant—branded. Because, to you, the lakou wasn't a society with a human face, a place of worship, an inheritance. It wasn't about spirituality, the philosophy of life, culture, respect for the elements, the affirmation of an afterlife and trajectories leading to it. Instead, it was, above all else, an enterprise, economically profitable, a tool of oppression you manipulated with a rare dexterity. I had no clue what to do with this name. By carrying it around, trying to understand circum-stances that inspired it, it found a place in my mind, like all the laws that had to be strictly observed, internalized. And so I didn't give it out, from the moment I realized someone couldn't be named what I was, even by mistake. I hid, searching for a long time behind the walls of anonymity, for someone, anyone . . .

ELEVEN

I don't have a job. It's all over, I said, because of my heroism. It's not every day that the insignificant puts an end to the grandeur of the almighty. Such an exploit warrants a good bottle of rum, which is what I rewarded myself with when I got home, after undressing, putting my suitcase down, folding my suit. I served myself generously and knocked back several others afterwards. I needed to celebrate it, and to calm my nerves a little bit . . .

At this moment, the city feels rather distant, and folks say that this doesn't bode well. What's clear is that misfortune creeps in through the silence, burning, killing, tracking its litany of blood, and then it disappears into oblivion . . .

The city holds its breath. Is it already aware of my defeat? Is it for or against me?

I have always been alone. I often pace around this room like a caged animal. Time stagnates, hardening like an immense, desiccated wall of stones on which a spectacle of shadows and nuances mingle amid hot, unbearable odours. An atrocious solitude. To the point of finding in them a source of comfort, of fellowship in the noises of the neighbours, in what the Other Within whispers to me. As a child, cradled in a bed of straw in the corner of the sheepfold where I slept alone, I was afraid the spirits of the lakou would come to imprison me forever in my sleep. The rustling of leaves. The chirping of crickets. The footsteps of the wind. The distant creaking of a door. To me, the realm of the night was a terrible tragedy. I still remember the evening when, terrified, I ran as fast as I could towards the kay mistè, to the room where I stumbled upon you, our Emperor, naked and surrounded by all the milk cows in the lakou. I was attached to a post, severely whipped at daybreak.

You punished us for no reason whatsoever, pou dan ri—just for kicks.

How could I survive until now in this immeasurable solitude? The solitude of a child who grew up somehow, for better or worse. Then the solitude of a man for whom tomorrow seems like another source of emptiness to avoid. A boss or an Emperor, it's the same evil, the same monster with a different face. The future, like the shivers of the city, gradually crumbles in the depths of anticipation . . .

TWELVE

The police have solved more difficult cases than this, ones where suspects flee, burrowing themselves into the most inaccessible places, even by foot. I'm not hiding. My pad is located a few blocks away from the police station. The street is like many others. Old. I believe the street was here before the city was born and started ignoring it, pushing it further away, until it was forgotten. The street fights back, clamouring from morning to night, runs away, gets into it, enough to drive a man crazy. Nothing like the neighbourhoods that enjoy a certain ease of living. The so-called safe neighbourhoods, so prim and proper— it's vulgar. In which men like me can only take out the trash and the stray dogs. To each their own life and death. Here, I have everything necessary for my solitude. The most basic of needs. A bed. Two chairs. A small table. The window has no use. It looks out to a wall. A sliver of a mirror that I never stare into any more for existential reasons. Everything is in its place. Even the cracked tiles seem to have been studied and planned.

One day I had seen nearly the same room, the same décor, on the cover of a school workbook I'd picked up somewhere. It was striking to see this image pasted there. And not some photo of a football star or a famous singer, as is so often the case, to send a clear message to the students, here are the models that we have to offer you, this is why you must continue going to school, because it's worthless. I took the workbook to my job and asked my Enlightened Colleague, a funny, witty man, 'Do you know who made this?'

'Who made what? This painting? Oh monsieur, it's a Van Gogh,' he said, without batting an eye, as he bound a stack of newspapers with string.

'It's written right there, *La Chambre à coucher* by Van Gogh.'

'*Vann Gwòg* . . . he sells rum?!'

'No, Van Gogh.'

'Who's that again?'

'A White man with an orange beard and a crazed face who painted so much of this stuff that it finally made him famous.'

His responses were always sharp and funny, sometimes he got carried away. I remember the first day, listening to the machines and the workers chatter away, my first question had been, 'How does this place work?'

'Oh monsieur'—as he almost always said at the beginning of his sentences—with the disconcerting naturalness that characterized him, 'it's a mass grave, the great survivor is the boss, we kill ourselves to fill his pockets.'

Through these few words, I understood that he didn't carry the boss in his heart, and that the boss must have been quite an asshole. And it immediately caused me to think about you . . .

THIRTEEN

You must be guilty to survive in this world.

You didn't work. The sheep were there for that. The life of an Emperor is the life of a dignitary, of an old hawk. Sit! Stand! Look down! Leave! Come back! Your orders poured down hard, unrelentingly. I repeat, the objective was to make me, to make all of us into a straight line, into zonbi. Beware of Emperors, whispered the Other Within, beware of all kinds of rulers, they reign for their own benefit—it's the most absolute truth. Orphans are easy prey, the ones who don't have shoulders large enough to carry their own dreams, their own pain. The Other Within, my one and only friend, told me to keep my eyes on the horizon, even in the dark, in this place deep inside myself, an unattainable refuge, far from imperial rigour. Everything preciously guarded, ripped from the world . . . *Hey, get up*! *Fetch me some tobacco*! You beat me. The little dusty creature (me) squirmed, pallid, and incapable of finding the strength within to obey. You struck again. *Get up, you little shit*! I managed to pull myself up by grabbing hold of the potomitan which, I must point out, had a photograph of the President of the Republic nailed to it, and I rolled out to fulfil my duty as a sheep. While you thought of names to call your dogs, scratched your ass and sniffed your fingers, your sheep rushed to your service, taking care of everything. Your food. Your laundry. Your bath. Your herbal tea. Your pipe. You were the master keeping an eye on the troublemakers in action, indefatigable, baking in the heat of the fields. Sheeplike figures labouring, harvesting, singing, exchanging glasses of kleren. Their ardour for work was incomparable. You demanded more than half the harvest, the cleanest, freshest water, the purest air, fire, the horizon. When you opened your eyes unto others, it was to ensure that they were always there, prostrate at your feet. The sheep formed a line, single file. Pushed at one another to offer you the fruits of their labour, proud to entertain the lwa, which they cannot see. Famished, preparing the banquet of the gods before returning to nibble the dust. 'May the gods eat and drink to satiation, to inebriation!' you cried out pompously. Animals recognize their own kind, consuming what they need to survive, contrary to you who devoured everything.

An enormous web of hypocrisy. This world where the gods—absences to which we accord infinite power—are explosives in the hands of mere mortals. Where human justice amounts to little more than crumpled paper next to that of the most passive and poorest among them . . .

FOURTEEN

Your heart is the drum of the gods, your eyes are their horizon, your soul is their fire in cold weather. I can still hear you going on about this nonsense while awkwardly guiding my hands over the drum with a dark and violent humour. If I gave the impression that I didn't feel anything you were saying, you would have cut me down with one blow. I didn't cry. That fanned your fury even more. It was like an affront. Mocking your power, your authority. You beat me again. *Dirty bastard*! It had nothing to do with the drum, or the fact that I didn't play it the proper way. If I had cried, you would have done the same to shut me up. Every path led to the violence of the character you embodied; the violence was limitless. Over time, I was no longer a human body, but a rubberized wall on which your blows, your Emperor's roars, came crashing miserably down. A time branded by hot iron, constant. Incidentally, the idea of leaving started to germinate, intensify long before all of this. Long before the Very Old Sheep told me the story of his life and that of the lakou. A life where everyone mattered (he kept insisting), and everyone had their place. The vèvè traced the geography of the future. The gods were watching, swearing while stomping the earth with their feet.

42

Never again would they allow the country to be stolen from them, to be reduced to slavery.

Being from nowhere, an orphan, I never cried at any point in my whole fucking life. Not once.

'Stick the drum firmly between your legs, you little shit! How many times do I have to repeat that!'

My role was precise. I was the only one who could fill it. I had large hands, made for this in a sense. Banging. Invoking. Amusing the spirits. They had decided. I was their drummer. Their appointed clown. One cannot escape their desires. But you knew it, too, this instrument was also a lie. And I was nobody. Those who, like you, glorify themselves to the point of believing themselves superior to others come from a broken genome, pre-tentious morons that should be eradicated, once and for all, before they invade every nook and cranny of Earth.

As for the drum and everything else, truth be told, I couldn't give a damn. I'll say it again, my only dream was to pull myself out of there, day by day, while your true face appeared to me as further evidence. The sombre desiccation of your heart. Forcing others into roles that benefitted you alone in the end. Not only did I find this abominable, but I didn't see the value in being a drummer above all else. I was stuck. From the beginning, I learnt against my will. Then, with time and the force of habit, I more or less acquired the dexterity necessary to continue alone. 'Open yourself up, be patient,' advised the Very Old Sheep in secret, 'become a receptacle, use your anger and strength.' Katap bitim plap bitim plap! The voice of the drum invites the voices of all Haitians and the other inhabitants of Earth to come together. The voice of the drum is one of the shared elements of our humanity. The voice of the drum carries us in it equally from every horizon of light. The Very Old Sheep had opened my mind. Attentive to the call of the open sea, my performances as an apprentice drummer continuously strayed from sacred and ritual dance rhythms so that I could express my depths, my secret trances. To get as close as I could to my own life. Projecting it beyond these lethargic skies, beyond any single thought. Yes, a personal quest. Otherwise, it made no sense to me. It was idiotic banging on a cowskin. Indenturing myself to the desire of things I do not believe in. In other words, I played for myself. I awakened the dogs within me. Arming them with growls, with all the depths of my lonely soul. Dogs are made to bark. To reach the breaking point, the firm border between night and day. To bite . . .

We're not at Carnival, you drum like you're told, or you get the fuck out of my ounfò, damn it!

My small liberties grated at you to the point where you could throw a tantrum in the middle of a ceremony, disturbing the Invisibles amid their slumber, overwhelmed by the heat and spicy peppers. Either I played according to your rules, or it was nothing at all. I had to watch my step, and stop embarking on journeys towards unknown realms.

The blind obedience to rules, to the detriment of the self, is the greatest of sins. It's a sheeplike passivity, death. Oblivion. The tightening of the body and soul around an unknown axis, murmured the Other Within, who carefully chose his moments to speak with me.

Wayward, rebellious, I started to beat my own drum again. To set out on an adventure. To follow my own meanderings, the secret pulse of the drum. The expanse of my dreams as well as its limits are infinite. Your increasing punishments didn't fix me or keep me on the straight and narrow. The pain washed over my body. The drum wasn't a drum any more, but a weapon, the contrary voice of the indignant.

'The instrument is not the path, the journey is within,' said the Very Old Sheep, pointing at his heart with his index finger, 'close your eyes . . .'

FIFTEEN

I hope I'll have the chance to get back to my Enlightened Colleague and my job. The memories in my head are jostling for position. They can be interrupted at any moment. Of the four or five pencil-pushing police officers in the station next door, none will risk pursuing someone who committed such an act. I imagine police with reinforcements arriving by car and motorcycle, pushing and shoving to get there in the nick of time, overpowering the guilty party who nevertheless awaits them peacefully. The street watches the national madness flair with anger and pity. Another production in the name of peace and security, some say. Instruments of lunacy, others think. The street and national madness are not of the same world. They have divergent interests. One proclaims its rights and inveighs against. The other beats, kills and demands silence in the name of power. For once it finds something better to do, the national madness doubles the pace—it sows panic through great means.

After the ceremonies, the participants, beguiled, threw me handshakes of wonderment here, of graciousness there. They congratulated me. The men said, you have a new world in your hands, son, you beat the drum like a god, keep it up. Bold and ripe women fluttered around me with full-lipped smiles. Folks saw a talent in me that I couldn't recognize. I couldn't help but be seen, appreciated for once. And to happily notice that the Emperor, the man who could speak to the dead and send the rain to weep somewhere else, the spiritual leader, was only entitled to a few nods of the head. The indications of your jealousy and your passion for dominance had been taken for a *thank you, monsieur, for allowing us to discover this little genius.* To be vaguely greeted after celebrating a sheep. The accolades and panegyrics I received, if they didn't require you to be indulgent towards me, were like a slap in the face. You must have felt so diminished, small, scandalized. The found child had grown up faster than you thought and hoped. The thought that one day I would replace you at the helm of the lakou, while your entombed body turned to rot, food for the worms, filled you with even more shadows. Upon the shepherd's death, a sheep succeeds him; now that's something we've never seen before. But the prospect of such a scenario could only leave indifferent an Emperor whose kingdom is only as big as his navel.

SIXTEEN

The last time I touched a drum was on a 6th of January. The day of the feast of the gods. The feast is dedicated to the great family of the Invisibles. This scandal could last for up to seven days. Seven days of debauchery and singing at the top of your lungs. Seven days of mysterious celebrations, tears, requests, thanks and explosions of joy. Seven days of making the drum hum, speak and sing the grandeurs of Vodou . . .

Meanwhile, the dawn—a rebellious and ochre halo, spilling over who knows what shore—softly crept through every pore of the night. Folks arrived gradually. Then it turned into an intense, motley crowd. Nobility. Believers. Non-believers. Doctrinarians. Oungan-in-training. Oafs. Wanderers. Seekers. The President of the Republic. The First Lady. Cabinet ministers and other civil servants. Senators. Deputies. Mayors. Section chiefs. Diplomats. Business leaders. Militants. Lovers of spectacle and flared emotions. Atheists. The curious. And so many others jockeyed with one another so that you could save themselves from their unjust, uncertain and miserable present, or so that you could tell them their future. A horde of dignitaries acting like plebes, insignificant, crying before a phony mystical leader—now that's a striking image.

Every year, on this date, they lusted after even more luck, power, everything, or they wished to partake in a leisure that was different from what they're normally exposed to in their milieu, and to set off once again in their armoured vehicles, causing the earth to shake. I heard it first from their accredited mouths that you were an Ati, the largest tree in the forest, the one that protects the smaller trees in foul weather, a supreme ruler. That this lakou, this filthy enclosure where time chases after its tail, bored to death, that this quagmire, this kiosk of corpses, was a tourist destination, a cultural patrimony, a mini museum, the sheep of the initiated, the zanj, and what else? Nonsense! They didn't place the offerings around the altar, nor did they chuck them in to the sacred source (a white enamel basin filled with water) that communicated with the sea and all other sacred sources all the way to Benin; they put them right into your hands . . .

A whole tide on the paved square where we welcomed the sable saints by hosing down the surroundings of the badji, specifically the entrance, with kleren, Florida water, ylang ylang, basil and other magical or attractive scents. The earth coiled around them. The sky appeared in the enamel basins. The gods mingled with the living. The charms resembled the corpses of children. The baobab was a powerful goddess, tall, adorned with all her jewellery, with dozens of breasts descending, heavy and smooth, like ripened fruit. A goddess indifferent to the half bows, flowers and magnanimity folks offered her. The earth became an inferno. Folks could barely speak or breathe. They were still pouring in, numerous, chosen, inspired, prodigious shadows returning to their native land expressly for the occasion. And these scenes never left me . . .

The sheep's dance: introduced by the hoarse sound of drums, perfumed, their heads tucked below a candle, all dressed in white, the initiated entered behind you one by one, each set down with devotion a plate of vegetables and seared fish glazed in honey on a mat at the foot of the potomitan. Masisi and madivin dancers paraded around in clothing either too tight or too big, disguised as false priestesses, pink panthers, flamboyant fairies or indulgent, callipygian sisters hustling and bustling, exaggerating their slightest gesture. The lwa love us as we are, proclaimed some with honey-soaked tones. A mistake of birth giggled others. Most of the time, these were pretexts to protect themselves from harsh masisiphobes, faceless and faithless anti-madivinity, and the hatred of monotheism. Preparing themselves for a trance with rhythmic and synchronized steps, they orbited the potomitan, symbolizing the axis of the world from the earth to the heavens, the plane between the visible and the invisible, the real and the unreal. You shook the ason, a tiny sacred toy, bellowing confused words. To open the gates of time leading to our world, you called upon Papa Legba. The master of keys and the heavens. With a single voice, the sheep gave the response in an impetuous, burning tongue, all while continuing their errantry. Supple, feverish strides, chests thrown in mid-air, rearing, shaking. Waves of hips and shoulders. Intemperate whirlwinds sweeping other bodies up in the trance, the crossroads between love and death sketched by the rum raining down on the battered earth of the temple. Onè, respè! Honour, respect! Legba made his entrance.

Ayibobo to welcome the afterlife—this was when I had to play hysterically. I beat the drum with a human femur. It's better with a bone, you explained, because it produces sounds that travel straight into the gods' ears. The initiated were now under the dominion of the afterlife: twisted, transported, pressed all together around the potomitan. Possessed, they were no longer themselves. Their entire universe churned in the storm that blew them, like reeds, in every direction. They flew from one abyss to another, winged and sublime. During almost the entire ceremony, a man chained the beaten, their feet buried beneath the soil, marionetted by the terrible Marinette Pye Chèch from the highest branch of the baobab. It was an unbelievable spectacle. Great art. An intense and spicy heat cleansed these perched bodies who appeared to be following a common quest, a common destiny, as though they were all there for each to con-tribute their stone to the edifice.

To refresh myself, an ewe brought me something to drink or blew alcohol into my face. Shivers took a hold of me each time, from my toes up to my eyes. 'The journey is within,' the Very Old Sheep's voice rattled around inside my head. And suddenly, I could no longer feel my hands or my body. Infinity and the oceans are a chronicle of childhood. Fucking hell! We're not at carnival here. Once again, I had to tidy up, forget my metaphors and return, as it were, to the sacred land. After a while, while a sheep stomped around a bonfire barefoot, crunching bits of burning wood along the way, they brought in a bull wearing a thong with a huge gold chain around its neck—Ogou Badagri. The thong belonged to Freda. The Ogou bull wore Freda's thong so that everyone would know, especially that bastard Agwe, that she was his wife and would not be anybody else's, even beyond eternity.

The morganatic wedding ceremony: through a range of processes and ritual gestures, you pretended to capture the attention of such-and-such spirit so you could invite him to unite with some happy mortal who, given the elevated costs of the ceremony, plus the rings, presents and other particular kindnesses for his supernatural companion, often burnt through his savings. In a word, he gave his soul to the lwa. And the new couple was, from then on, linked by a common fate.

Divine punishment: the blasphemers, little knuckleheads chuckling during the celebration, sometimes going as far as to help themselves to the dried fruits, grilled corn and peanuts offered to the spirits of the dead who dare not enter, were punished in the most unbelievable fashion. You were the only one capable of forgiving them. No one else was authorized to complete this task, which was both a wonder and a farce. But, once again, this was only a lure. There wasn't any cabalistic punishment, or anything else. You would arrange for someone to act like a pain in the ass, pretending to have been bound, for example, by a common vine from which he couldn't manage to break loose. Then, you came over and broke the unbreakable bind before the eyes of the simultaneously terrified and fascinated spectators.

The lucky mud: a thick and black mud the sheep rolled around in, clinging to one another in an orgiastic scene, spraying rum or the blood directly from the slit throat of a quality rooster, at times murmuring, at others bellowing laments and prayers . . .

The grande toilette: with one hand, they washed their genitals with the juice of goat peppers, and with the other, they emptied an entire bottle of kleren in one go, without breathing. No pain, no particular discomfort could be read on their faces.

The blessed bread: 'Ahhhhh! They're chewing shards of glass bottles!' one spectator reluctantly screamed, distraught.

Nemesis: condemned by the maniacally depressive gods to feel the effects of their demented ablutions, of their excesses, the sheep were writhing on the ground. Screaming. Imploring. Their suffering was indescribable . . .

SEVENTEEN

A whole life devoted to evil, built on the slipping sands of your affectation. Your Victorian armchair. Imperial habits. Your enormous rings. Your pointy Crakows. Your rainbow-coloured kerchiefs. Your stilted, precious air of understanding the depths of images and feelings. The tobacco powder you inhaled. The sacred hiccup. The loaded altar. The enamel basin overflowing with cowries, reminding us of our enslaved ancestors. The thunderstones. The vèvè, the spirits' itineraries. The drapo revealing a grouchy sun, upon closer inspection, a grotesquely made-up woman's head in the middle of two interlaced serpents. The feathery jars. The various faces, profiled, like clippings of dreams. The masks. The sequins. The sacrificed beasts. The blood, never enough to quench the gods' thirst. Your hyperbolic decrees. Ex cathedra tartines, the meaning of which escaped me. All this ridiculous staging, this act, to give the impression that you were someone you had never been. A champion of magic and occult passions. An Emperor deserving of his title, who never left anything to chance, in balance between personal harmony and cosmic energy. No noble of an ancient nation handed down the arson to you at the stroke of midnight. You were far from a

Ti Ginen. A propitiatory soul. A mage of unsurmountable skill. A healer. A practitioner. A shaman. An heir. A fortress. The preferred lover of the three Egyptian women. The star of David. A refined connoisseur of unknown worlds. A talented diviner of an infallible, cultivated flair, acting in the name of a geometric certainty of the present and the future, mastering the language and the secret fluctuations of dreams and their reverberations. A Gran Mèt who lives many lives at once, as well as out-of-season lives; one who knows how to wed actions to words, to enact justice, to read the immensity of the most distant margins, to incarnate the spirits and is familiar with their favourite colours, their rhythms, their alcohol and the order in which they appear and take their seats at the ceremonial table . . .

In the history of the Spirits, never had they been so unjustly called upon, roped in, debased. You held the keys to nothing. There was no therianthrope or nocturnal tarsier, which was supposedly your animal form, or some other chimera creeping through the night towards the day. The beribboned black bottle hanging from the mapou didn't contain any virtuous, vigilante saviour zonbi, but rather the smoke that you sold to lost folks looking for fast and easy solutions. These souls, suspended or seated at the entrance to the store or the family house, can perform miracles. For example, luring in the clientele, causing their business to flourish. Elevating the limp dick of an impotent man. Bestowing children upon a sterile woman. Encouraging an adulterous husband or wife to return to the family hearth.

Working hectares of land in one single evening. Bringing death upon the enemy . . . You had zero power, and you knew it all along. You were nothing more than an ignoramus, a moron forsaken by all.

EIGHTEEN

Knock, knock, knock!

They're knocking blindly. If it's not the right door, they move onto the next. One time, there was even one who got his ass beat by a hysterical tenant. Echoes of the tussle made the rounds. This building is a nightmare. Nine floors. Confusing hallways. Never-ending doors. Most of them tagged, riddled with holes. Behind each of them a wicked story is brewing. The most well-known and talked about is the one about the musician who fell into decrepitude after a stroke. He had the bad habits of a tortured artist. He couldn't help himself. He'd leave the stage in the middle of a concert to do drugs. He lived the beautiful life until the fall sent everything crashing down. Ruined by his infirmity and the exorbitant cost of certain treatments, the Haitian star had become a pile of bones laid out on a fetid sheet amid his prizes, awards, portraits and CDs. The little old lady who comes by every day to take care of him told me the whole thing. Life is a ball, my boy, today it rolls for you, tomorrow it'll roll for someone else . . .

On the floor above, feet stomp so hard that I'm not sure what the floor is waiting for to fall on my head.

Somewhere in another room, there's a story collector. Having heard there is no one else like her for people to confide in, I suspect she knows nearly everything about the whole building. She came a-knocking once or twice to see if there was anything I wanted to talk about. 'You're the only person whom I know nothing about.' She asked about my life, my job. 'I like getting to know people,' she insisted.

I refused, telling her, 'I'm not interested in what you're selling, leave me be.' At the same time, there's a baby screaming while its parents argue, causing furniture, glasses and kitchen utensils to fall to the floor . . .

The city is eclipsed by the night, clinging to the same attitude. A spontaneous distance. Anyway, she couldn't do anything for me, this urban imposture. The die have been cast. That said, I've seen that bitch behave in execrable ways to defend notorious criminals, and worse. Me, I'm nobody, and I have no use for her largesse. The idea of leaving this place with my hands cuffed behind my back, all beaten up, to be locked up half a despicable square metre was becoming increasingly more acceptable as I wandered through my memories . . .

NINETEEN

My time is running out. But I want to return to the one you called the 'Stranger', the one who, in the language of mysteries, doesn't talk or do anything besides observe, learn and bend to the rites of the household. I'm aware of the lengths you go to veil the truth about him. I remembered it as soon as I turned the story collector away. Before she left, she said, 'The Haitian star has fallen.' The little woman, her mistress, had come to collect his belongings. In my opinion, it's for the best. How atrocious, having to wallow in your own shit . . .

You dozed beneath the baobab while an enormous, hairy spider, that was also a Vodou spirit, wandered about the branches. The men slaved away in the fields. The women hurried to cook your food, to run your scented bath and whatnot. Your slightest demands were heard and attended to as quickly as possible. The kids had just discovered a new game which consisted of blowing dust in each other's eyes. Either I take part in the game and leave a minute later screaming, blind, with my face in my hands, or succumb to my boredom, simmering in my disgust for everything. Once again, the sky decided not to fall on top us and put an end to this shitty existence, when the silhouette of a man appeared on the horizon. The Stranger seemed to come from far away, from another tale, as if called upon by Bawon Samdi himself in this graveyard of sheep on the path of a lost memory. The wind picked up. The more he explained himself, the more his mystery intensified. He wore simple and dirty clothing, with a fabric satchel like a bandolier. His gaze projected a wound, a glassy dream. Was he an exhausted hero seeking respite or a sorcerer fleeing heavenly vengeance?

You jumped when you saw him, nearly falling out of your chair. Even the domestic spider-lwa reacted in a strange way, as though both of you had seen death itself. 'The gods welcome you into their home,' you promptly said to the Stranger. Your voice was wavering, revealing great inner turmoil. It was curious, the Emperor, the grand spiritual leader, was no longer himself in the presence of this poor man. We could see it clearly, with a simple glance, he stripped you of your clothing, demystified your excursions, your bloody harvests, the meaning hidden behind your six fingers, the bizarre gashes covering your lonely, artificial pine-tree skin. 'I'll get you some coffee!' There's always an abundance of coffee in the pot on the eternal flame.

'No thanks,' the man said.

'We aren't allowed to refuse the nerves of the gods, etc.' you responded.

The man ultimately accepted, drinking a cup. The forced labour shimmered from afar, indefatigable—*travay n ap travay* o! *Oh, we're working all the livelong day*! The sky above them was the clearest blue, bereft of any birds or nuance. I couldn't take my eyes off you, at the same time I cautiously avoided being seen. I was impatient to learn more about this Stranger who apparently wasn't as strange as you would have hoped. Your enigmatic humour, your slightest gestures hinted at the fact that you didn't think you'd see him so soon, or perhaps ever. 'I think this dude is here to reveal some grand truth about the Emperor,' the Other Within shot back. Then, you invited the man to lunch.

Apart from political men, high-society businessmen and other clothed infections, nobody was allowed to sit next to you at the oak table in the middle of the terrace to the kay-mistè, neither for coffee, nor to eat. It was necessary to understand that the favourable treatment of the Stranger, despite his looks, meant he was important. Nothing less would have warranted your benevolence and acts of grace. At that very moment, a sheep came bearing bad news. Something horrible had happened to a friend. He was bleeding to death. Without letting him finish, you sent him packing. You didn't want to hear it. You had important matters to handle. The Stranger deserved your undivided attention. From the terrace, a hallway led to the private sections of the house. Lunch was nothing more than a ruse aimed at drawing the man into your lair, the place where profane eyes and ears were not supposed to penetrate, passing the banquet hall where two tables overflowed with food the gods apparently hadn't touched. It's clear, this man didn't show up here randomly, I mumbled to myself in response to what the Other Within had just whispered to me. I must remember, you were prepared to do anything to protect your lies. And that day, more than ever, they appeared to be in great danger. All the same, I had to confirm my suspicions. Risking my own safety, I seized a moment of inattention, slipped into your bedroom through the back door and hid myself under your bed. The cement was cold. I tried to relax as much as possible to avoid trembling and throwing myself foolishly into the wolf's mouth. In front of me, hanging on the wall, I noticed an enormous coat. I found the presence of this garment intriguing in such a place.

Suddenly, you entered the bedroom with the Stranger. Since his arrival, he hadn't understood why you were acting bizarrely around him. You sternly asked him to zip it, to leave the lakou immediately.

'What the fuck is your problem?!' the man shouted. 'Are you kidding or do you really not recognize me?! I'm your fucking brother, look, it's me! And what's all this?' With a sweeping gesture, his body followed his arms left, and then right, with a pretentious air. 'Why did you hold onto this coat? What are you still cooking up in this forgotten dump? Have you gone mad?'

'No,' you replied, 'but you, you were a former prisoner. Get out, there's no room for you here.'

'Because of you, I lost years of my life,' the Stranger shot back, 'and this is how you treat me, you're a dirty traitor.'

The man left the bedroom and flipped over the banquet table, scattering the sacred food across the floor . . .

In the days following your reunion, loads of questions, hypotheses and visions scurried about in my mind. I thought about what the past must have been like for the two of you. I tried to guess the reasons why we had never seen him before, this brother of yours. We knew nothing about his existence, why did he suddenly appear at this moment and not before? I tried to piece together the story with the shards of your conversation. But years would go by before I would understand the scene I had just witnessed.

TWENTY

There it is. The stomping above and shouting on the other side of the wall continues. *Motherfucker! You only care about your mistresses! You're letting our child to starve to death. Shut up! Stupid whore!* The baby was crying. The wife, too. It's unbearable. We shouldn't ever have neighbours, friends or people who buzz around us like flies. I don't think it's normal. My experience has taught me that when a simple courtship becomes a relationship, whether friendship or love, it can only end in failure. We want to feel transported by the idea that life has a higher meaning when we're in a couple, but it's not true. In a couple, we're nobody. I want to be myself, full stop! The people in the building watch me, I watch them, and that's enough for me. It should be enough for them, too. But you know what, goddammit, there's always someone ready to stop you in your tracks, like this woman collecting stories. If I wanted someone to talk to, to confide in, it would definitely be my Enlightened Colleague because he's not looking to be my friend, he's looking for nothing at all. I ask him a question, he responds, sometimes without even looking at me, then he continues doing what he was doing, and that's it . . .

Regarding the Stranger, the Very Old Sheep mumbled his conclusion—'He shouldn't have come here, he's leaving with a cadaver hanging over him, forever . . . I no longer know how to make myself useful. But I'll never take an oath of allegiance to this masquerade . . .'

'What was that noise?' interrupting himself abruptly to lend an ear.

'Are you sure the Emperor isn't close by?'

'No. He's in the middle of a conversation with the dangling spider.'

'That piece of shit spider! An idle lwa! Very well, then I'll continue. My God, at the same time, there's not much left in my mind either. When I think about it some more, I feel waves in my stomach. It was a difficult time. The dust blinded us. No amount of prayer could blow it away. Everything around the sanctuary was dying, the earth, the water, the trees, the birds. The gods distanced themselves from us. There are some that never returned.'

The Very Old Sheep confessed to me that, for the first time, his faith was being tested. Our suffering was not complete; freshly arrived from who knows what pit, the Emperor abused us, imposed laws on us, gagged everyone in the name of the same gods that we'd lost sight of for some time, since the beginning of our misery. I had recognized that he was not the person he was pretending to be, but an out-and-out liar, a hypocrite. Vodou is my life. I can spot a non-believer from kilometres away, without asking him to state the identity of all the gods in the pantheon, to trace me a vèvè on the ground or to hum a Chante Lwa, a

Vodou song. The problem is, when he's unmasked, he has no other recourse than cruelty, prepared to do anything to further his existence, to justify his perversity. You must respect nature and the order of things; you cannot consider one (based on personal need or not) and reject the other. If you don't have any cards left in your hand, for example, how can you, in concrete terms, play a round with a friend or obtain clarity, explain a situation or reveal the future? Without a lakou, there's no community and no religious life. Without a drum, there's no sèvis lwa, no ceremony. Without a guide, there's no family, no nation. So, when it started getting out of hand, becoming unbearable, I said it's not right, I don't agree, the lwa don't ask for that, for us to crush our neighbours, for us to reduce them to slavery, not for anything! I had insisted. What else could I have done? We would have had to shout him down, chase him off immediately, from the very first day, all together in agreement. I had already become a faulty engine, rusted away by the accumulation of worries, the force of which was like a reed weathering the storm, then I became a nuisance, a grouch, like a prayer the gods no longer listen to, you've got to silence him, that's the only way. One evening, a shadow entered the sheepfold, shook me, awakened me. I stood up to see who it was. It sprayed me with sulfuric acid, and since then the light in me died out. My life unfolds in complete darkness, lost.

The baby started crying again.

TWENTY-ONE

Certain people, especially the blind champions of Vodou, the profoundly illuminated, will find the portrait I've painted of you nothing more than an attempt to sully the name of our dear country, offending the memories of our ancestors. All that I'm saying, and I'm convinced, is that the sacred justifies the best and the worst of human behaviour—it just so happens that my experience was forged by the latter.

I left with these words of the Very Old Sheep in my mind: 'The future will not stop here, my son, according to the signs of the fâ, but, beyond these sad peaks and valleys, there is a world, more than a world. Perhaps there is a life for you there, go ahead before it's too late.' The Master is right, the Other Within went so far to say.

I hopped on the bus without asking myself where it was headed. I had long dreamt of this moment. Breaking free of the cage. I still look back on those memories of the smell of alcohol, hot peppers, sweat. These phantasmagoric images of possessed humans, riding it out, dead drunk. These sheep that we found rigor mortis in the mud after a stormy night. And, of course, that time when you threw me into your bedroom, pressed my shoulders into the floor, shoved your unsheathed dick into my face, ordered me to suck you off, again and again and again, fuck! We don't deny the Spirits anything. Then you forced my legs open and stuck a finger in my ass, before penetrating me with all your power as an Emperor. All this while reminding me with a pontificating voice that here the masisi and madivin will find grace in the eyes of the pantheon, the same as anyone else, as you accelerated your thrusts. My insides were opening up. I pissed myself and vomited simultaneously. My vision blurred. I could no longer breathe. Dirty little snot, clean up your vomit! No, not with your hands. With your tongue, quickly! Now, get out! You put away your dick and life continued. The traces of blood from my violation confirmed divine satisfaction. I should consider myself lucky to have pleased them.

It kept happening. And more than once I pondered suicide. I was convinced that it was the only way to get rid of these images in my head. I decided to do it, but when the time came to act, I couldn't. All I'd have to do was climb the baobab with a rope in the middle of the night and that'd be it. The gods called him home, that's probably all you would have found it necessary to say, finding my body undulating in the dawn, before assembling the sheepfold for a farewell ceremony, then the beautiful burial. I would have missed the bus to my childhood, and that would have been it for me.

If only you could imagine the gaping wound you left in me. The gods, no more than a metaphor for your perversity, they must have realized that I was a defenceless adolescent, easy prey. But you set about transforming the whole world into an immense infection, and they would say nothing, those eternally passive beings, no, they wouldn't hold you back.

That day on the bus, for the first time in my life, I felt alive. The smell of fresh air. Life as it was meant to be lived. Without getting slapped around, or being constantly squashed . . .

For a normal sheep, my actions were unnatural. How can I put it? Whatever happens, you never turn your back like that on the lakou, we're all there because the earth and the gods will it, not because of our own free will . . .

I'll never look back. The gods never needed me. Nor I them.

TWENTY-TWO

The bus from my childhood didn't travel too fast, nor too slow. The lakou became a clouded memory, a place removed from reality. Your voice got quieter and quieter as I moved forward in my life as a free man.

She was seated next to me with an old book in her hand. A beautiful woman, confirmed the Other Within. Transported by her reading, only her body remained there, slender, while her mind drifted elsewhere. She wore a turquoise dress. She had multicoloured eyes. One black, the other chestnut. Her ebony hair was held up by a crocodile-shaped clip. Her presence, agreeable and practically enigmatic, disturbed me. All of a sudden, I felt a sort of heat wave in the pit of my stomach, in my mind and in my legs. Something inexplicable that I believed to be ephemeral—after seeing her, the rest of the world had become a vast silhouette. I also couldn't keep myself from being intrigued by this strange book whose yellowed pages were dotted by little stains and frayed around the edges. Certain pages had come unglued. When the time came to flip to the next one, she did it so slowly, with so much precaution, that you'd think she wouldn't be able to turn the page. The shaking caused by the road didn't make her task any easier. Who is she? I asked myself.

I still wonder. Where is she from? What about this book can be so interesting, so necessary, that one could get so lost in its pages? She guessed my wonder, my presence in search of hers. From the side of the road where I waited alone, I thought that she drew herself in closer, while the bus barely slowed down long enough for me to place my foot and climb on board.

The name I carry today, I owe it to her, a real woman. Not some woman with downcast eyes that you force into your bedroom. A million lit candles, a mountain of incantations recited with the greatest fervour wouldn't suffice to make her submit to your tyranny. She would have been capable of withstanding your gaze. Putting your legends, the vapours of your Black pantheon and your crushing verticality in their place. Restoring your human condition. You would have wanted to punish her. To inflict upon her the worst humiliations, tying her to a post, for example, to whip her again and again, leaving her body and mind with scars to last forever before running her off and regaining your rocking chair with your pipe and your jug of kleren in the benevolent shade of the baobab . . . A drafty name, naked and sombre all at once.

You might find it bizarre, a little far-fetched, but I knew that I had just had a unique encounter. I already cherished it. I enjoy showing up somewhere and not knowing what will happen, you watch, you listen, you learn, and then, one day, you become like a fish in water.

'Where are you headed?' she asked me, without taking her head out of her book. Followed by these words that I found so apt, 'You're travelling empty-handed?' Truth be told, I had five thousand goud in my sock. A sum that I had accumulated with the tips left by my former admirers during my drum performances.

'I don't know,' I replied, 'wherever the bus wants to leave me.'

'It stops in the city.'

'Well then, that's perfect for me. I've never set foot in a city before.'

'It's a shame how all dreams head to the city in the hopes of coming true.'

With an air of sadness, she sighed as she closed her book. 'To set out, leave it all behind, to reinvent yourself.'

Memories are the hardest to manage. Nobody knows what to do with them. She shared other things about herself with me. She liked tea, books, of course, and travelling around, deep into the countryside. There's a profound spiritual, cultural and ecological wealth to behold and to protect. She said this with a lassitude that challenged the negligence of political leaders and other reckless people. All of a sudden, almost automatically, images flashed before my eyes of the amulets destined to be sold, made from the last of the trees bordering the lakou, images of mysterious trucks you made us fill with vetiver, sisal, coffee and so on for the scraps the other vultures through your way.

I asked her if it wasn't too difficult to move around like that when you have a family and all (in truth, I wanted to know if she was single, available). As I'd hoped, she wasn't married, didn't have any children, nor did she have much luck with men. These last words were followed by a moment of silence. More than a moment of silence, the scent of a painful, unsinkable past. She didn't seem too surprised when I told her that I didn't know how to read or write. It must have come out of my mouth as though I'd hoped to explain myself. But that wasn't it. I didn't know what else to say. She smiled and said, 'I'm sure it's not your fault. You know, we're not always responsible for who we are or what happens to us. And what we call intelligence, the secret light that animates us from within, it's not the providence of princes and kings, it lies within . . .' She put me at ease, but not being used to conversing with a woman, one who was of such a beauty, that compensated for my muddled feelings. In other words, I wouldn't have opened myself up. I wouldn't have confessed anything to her. These things, I don't know, you keep them to yourself. It was harder to say my name. I didn't have one yet. Let's just say that my name before was everything but a name, a true name. Especially because, ever since I left the lakou, I've never met someone who was called by their birthdate or a god's favourite number. Anyway, this sudden intimacy enflamed a host of feelings in my mind, some sweeter, more intoxicating than others. No other being had ever pleased me, possessed me, as much as she did . . .

She was taken from me, and as a result, thick shadows seized hold of me. And someone simply got what they deserved.

There's still stomping above me. The baby's not crying any more. The voice of the story collector goes, 'A life story told never has an ending . . .'

TWENTY-THREE

For too long, my feet lost the urge to walk. To be free, feet are made to wander, to be put to use. My eyes pored over the closed horizon to the baobab, from the bleak misery of the sheep in their huts to the morose colours of the sky, looking for a sign that never came. I pulled at my skin with all my strength, it imprisoned my dreams. As soon as I saw this city, I knew it was what I needed after so many years of seclusion. Come and go as I please. Complete anonymity. It was all over for me, obedience to a boss, the ceremonies, the drum. I've beat the drum a few times since, but only in my dreams where everything unfolds in the past or in a very distant old age. I avoided everything that could have reminded me of what I had been. I needed to reinvent myself and start living right away.

'Port-au-Prince, end of the line!' shouted the conductor. To say goodbye, she reached out her hand. I hesitated. Then grabbed a hold of it, this hand of an unrivalled softness that I could still feel, long after her taxi melted into the city's mass. Meanwhile, I turned around in circles, lost and distressed.

The contrast between the days before, that day, and those that followed was troubling. In the end, I left the land of wind, plains and mountains as far as the eye can see for this cauldron of things, of bodies towing their lives behind them like a heavy burden beneath a white-hot sun. An immense lakou ravaged by deprivation and selfish madness. Abundant absences. But who knows where water goes to wet the geraumon's feet.

A few months later, I was hired as a delivery man for the country's leading daily newspaper. I was lucky. God knows the trials of the destitute—those who don't matter, don't know anyone, have no patrons. More than half the city is looking for work and have never worked in their lives. I figured this was no reason to stand idly by with my arms crossed.

After a few hours in an overly air-conditioned room, seated before the conceited gaze of two ungracefully aged and completely over-made-up receptionists you would have thought were ugly corpses, the boss himself arrived in flesh and blood, greying, paunchy, deep into his sixties, wearing blue slacks and a pink shirt. When he saw me, a rictus of confusion appeared on his enormous face, as if to say, why not smile at this poor loser if it makes him feel better, if it makes him feel like he knocked at the right door, like he was standing in the presence of some guardian angel—why not? People have an unhealthy belief in what they desire, in what soothes them. There's nothing you can do to fight this illusion. He studied me from head to toe. 'You're skinny,' he directed at me with disaffection, 'but you're young and you have long legs, which is to your advantage, because it's a job for walkers, the indefatigable.' He also talked about punctuality, organization, rigour and risks.

'I can walk forever and very quickly,' I offered pathetically. 'Where I come from, we have to walk kilometres in search of water.'

'And where do you come from?'

I didn't know how to answer this question. I didn't know where I came from. I had never heard anyone speak the name of the place in Haiti where the lakou could be found. But that didn't seem to interest the boss that much anyway. If I hadn't said that last stupid sentence, he wouldn't have asked me a thing. 'Well,' he said, 'you'll have to be able to recall a ton of addresses at the drop of a hat.'

'I have a good memory, monsieur.'

He called someone and ordered him to explain everything in further detail.

'Thanks, boss!'

Filled with an infallible sense of hope, I was suddenly no longer thirsty, no longer hungry. I felt like a thousand men. I must admit that from the first encounter, I could tell that I was in the presence of a very refined and pretentious man. I said as much, the boss was among the first subjects I broached with my Enlightened Colleague. 'The boss, do you know him well? What's he like?'

'Oh, monsieur,' he replied . . . He had clearly answered this type of question before and confirmed the apprehensions of the new recruits. 'Oh monsieur, what is sure, the little I know about him, is that he's no fun at all, he treats his partners like shit, runs them out in the middle of meetings to greet his mistresses—and he has more skirts than he does shirts. He's a pervert. He manipulates people for pleasure, trapping them and putting them into extremely humiliating situations. It must get him really riled up and boost his sense of superiority. One time, he called me into his office, and congratulated me on my hard work and expertise before offering me a promotion. He looked very serious. I was happy. It was good news for me, you know. A promotion is something unheard of in the life of a delivery man. While walking out, overcome with joy, he lashed out like a whip at my back, "Wait a second, I'm sorry, it's a mistake, we don't have any vacancies for the job I just gave you, in fact, the job doesn't even exist! Ha, ha, ha, I'm just messing with you! Damn, that was a good one, right? I love messing around—oh no, don't tell me that you actually believed me! Well, go ahead, please close the door behind you . . ." There's the answer to your question, that's the kind of guy the boss is.'

TWENTY-FOUR

'A man without a job is like a boat without a rudder, or a ship-wreck,' said the Very Old Sheep. I loved sharing my happiness with him. This yoke of misery was my Our Father, my Hail Mary, my Dahomey, my four hundred and one lwa, my twenty-one nations, my painful bread, my enraged drums in the heart of bodies, my trance.

Imagine a long hallway full of men, not one single woman, half-asleep, bent over, barely supporting themselves, ravaged by the boredom and bitterness of a lifetime, revenants, lost at sea, unravelled. This hallway of goats for the slaughter. There were also young graduates, ulcerated by their National Education, builders in whom people entrust the construction of nothing any more, disappointed and resigned, with much less than they're worth so that they don't die, their eyes full of shame.

This hallway led to the machine room where the newspaper was produced. Long after we've finished printing it, the whirring lingered in our heads, like the barking voice of the foreman, pul-ling us out of our somnolence—jounal la parèy! The newspaper's ready! We move our asses. Everyone grabs a bundle and throws himself into the mouth of the street. Time passes by. The routine sets in.

Five o'clock in the morning. The streets are still empty and suspect. I've seen them in all their configurations. The most gorgeous rosary of stars in magical sunrises. Under attack by firearms, when the armed gangs go at it prodigiously. The fear of getting stranded on a dead-end street during a delivery made my guts churn. There are some delivery men who, after getting attacked or witnessing something they shouldn't have, preferred to rot in unemployment, without a penny to their name, dying of hunger. Being a newspaper delivery man in this city, like many jobs, was like walking a tightrope over an abyss. What's more, I delivered mainly in the neighbourhoods with the worst reputations. The question that kept coming back to me was this, how could people living in material conditions as hard as these read? It's surprising but true, affirmed my Enlightened Colleague, the readers of the newspaper are the poor, the paupers, the good-for-nothings, us, the eternal dreamers. The rich are a bunch of sharks, risk takers who only swear by profit. We're paid nothing to enrich them even further. Delivering their lies. Their dolled-up schemes. Their smoky measures. The enticing opportunities offered to the winners. The Unavoidable Death to the losers. In any case, it's easier to sit back in your armchair and leaf through the polluted air of the times than it is to stick your nose outside and attempt to change them. These are the analgesic writings the watchdogs of the status quo use to brainwash us, to crush us, to jettison us all . . .

My Enlightened Colleague was furious about everything. I'm surprised that he didn't do what I did before me—only, would he have had the courage to wait for the police to arrive? I understood his anger. To me, the newspaper wasn't the right place for him, considering his knowledge and lucidity. But is there a place in this country for those who are angry, who refuse to accept injustice and the sanctioned moral order? Where corruption and impunity stand as institutions among others. And, on the strength of their parliamentary pleasantries, feeble politicians force-feed us lies. Parlay us into nothing. Fill us with rage. Search for ways to kill us even more. In the most spectacular way possible. They're paid for it with our money, our sweat, our blood. Flaunting our foundational liberties. Trampling our laws. Nobody trusts anyone any more. We have nothing left. It's anarchy. A blind search for personal glory. The sanctioning of ignorance, rape, death, putrefaction and hellfire. An ungoverned country. The President of the Republic dropped his pants to moon the children of a village that had never seen an official's ass. A beautiful, public ass. 'The coffers of the state are empty,' he bemoaned. From the street, we saw him wiggling his hips in his office to the rara music played by those protesting his political regime. During the opening of a sidewalk that had cost the state a goldmine, he reiterated his promise to continue pushing the country down the path of development. Millions of green dollar bills disappeared into shell companies and dead-end contracts. On an official visit to a large European city, he declared this, 'If my political adversaries in Haiti knew how good I have it here, they would take advantage of my absence to foment a coup d'état. This one senator is a car thief and a kidnapper. And from time to time, random stories are every bit as good as the great catastrophes that surpass them. A motorcyclist is caught in the act with a cadaver on his bike. A battered woman ended up stabbing her husband. She cooked up his body and invited over the neighbours who brought their appetites. The body of a young girl was found on top of a pile of trash, the latest in a long list. Armed bandits divide up the day and the night. The Minister of Justice took a year-long sabbatical to brainstorm a new way of ordering justice. Political discourse closely resembles a religious message; we don't know what's hidden beneath the surface, or how much it concerns us, and everyone is capable of the unexpected in order to defend their own truth. In short, this country is a sea of shit. A tomb. For those of whom it represents an opportunity, a liveable place, they're not from here and they know nothing about it except through their shady mission or their petty pleasures. Without mentioning the wealthy who do nothing but pig out and pig out some more . . . As if all you had to do was pinch your nose for carrion to turn into ham. And anonymous, invisible heroes, who sacrifice themselves to achieve beautiful things that nobody will recognize, that you won't read about in any newspaper. In short, we live in a black hole. We'd all leave if we could, every single one of us.'

TWENTY-FIVE

Depending on the month, the season, the news, they entrusted me with a bundle of a hundred or a hundred and fifty papers, and all of them had to be delivered by 9 a.m. The boss was clear, if a subscriber drinks their coffee without their paper, it means that the paper might as well cease to exist. We've always got to be at the top of our game . . .

Despite the poor working conditions, between the guardians of the night we were more or less solid, especially in the secrecy of ill-gotten gains. For example, before going home, a delivery man had to report the subscriber's fees to the newspaper's accounting division. An ill-conceived or deliberately designed system meant to tempt us, or to test our good faith. From time to time, some of us went outside of the rules and kept the money, alleging that we had been held up by bandits. Oh, no way monsieur, we're not stealing from the rich. We're taking back a speck of dust from what they've swindled. We owe them no such gratitude . . .

We were so underpaid that we avoided talking about our salaries, which only served to settle the debts we had accumulated. Our ill-gotten gains rounded out the last days of the month. I did it five or six times. The deduction my Enlightened Colleague took was fair. The rich are the thieves, the crocodiles, murderers, the official sponsors of the war, the dictatorship, the producers and exporters of inequalities, the owners of heaven and Earth. We're their doormats, their circus animals, their bloodhounds, their bulletproof vests, their niggers. Admiring the boss' pennies, I wondered why we did what we were doing, we took all the risks, and we had to steal just to find out what a measly salary looked like. I immediately stopped skimming, terrified that one day I might have to own up to my actions. Some didn't take it well. 'This country uncovers one crisis to cover up another,' I argued in my defence, 'life gets increasingly more expensive and insignificant, right guys? At some point, you've got to stop, think for a second and quit playing around.'

I needed to hang onto this job, even if to do so I had to go all out, expose my vulnerabilities, embody something greater than bravery. The simplest delivery is a race against the clock. The risks appear according to the city's changing mood. Streets flooded, blocked, littered with trash, dead bodies, discouraged by newspaper headlines. The splashing mud and the enormous whirlwinds of dust kicked up by passing cars. The odious clientele. In these conditions, who can move faster than time? But my boss, as far as his business kept going, he didn't give a shit. One time, I don't remember any more which one of us mustered enough courage and took it upon himself to reveal the difficulties of our mission. A car, monsieur, a motorcycle, even a bicycle would make things easier on us, the delivery man nearly begged. The big fatso looked at him from head to toe before stating that his family had run this business for more than a century and that there was no need for all these gadgets, at least here we pay you on time, the mailmen can't even say as much. Then he demanded that this idiot get out of his sight if he didn't wish to regret his stupidity.

The boss maintained that you needed a sturdy set of legs, but what you needed more than anything else was high spirits. In spite of that, I did a good job, I gave it my all. Only, a few weeks before my masterpiece—you've got to be a real artist to achieve something with as much finesse as I did—the consequences of which couldn't wait to set in, I scratched myself often and violently. I had a hard time falling asleep, tormented by random thoughts, and at the end of my existential wading pool, when my nerves calmed down, I let myself drift into a hypothetical somnolence. Oh shit! It was already time to go hang in the printing hall. Against my better judgement, I decided to stumble in. Behind my eyes, when I closed them, surged a bloodred heatwave. I could barely make out the disappearing night. Each of my steps demanded enormously painful concentration. You would've thought I was living out the last pages of my life. Often too weighed down, exhausted, when the news, impetuous and searing, spilled loads of ink and folks grew more interested in the newspaper than usual, I had no other choice than to chuck copies of the newspaper into the sewers, over the first fences I could find by the twos, threes—it didn't matter—or I took the remaining papers home with me, and then I used it to fulfil many functions, including to wipe my ass.

TWENTY-SIX

The night was dragging its final puffs of mist, dark, erubescent blue and burnt topaz. Here, the nighttime always seems to stalk, carefree, like a bird of prey.

While I hurried to get to work, a shadow jumped out in my direction. It moved quick, hard and resolute, as though carved in stone. Once in front of me, it whipped something out. A gun, a knife. I couldn't tell. It told me to put my hands in the air. Pushed me against the wall. Took my wallet, my shoes, an old bracelet made of pyrite that someone had sold me as though it were real gold, to the point of forcing me into an alley to finish me off for good, when all of a sudden two other shadows came along. Startled, my assailant mumbled 'It's your lucky day, motherfucker,' and then disappeared.

At a wealthy home (the only one on my list), an evil woman unleashed her hounds on me. I had to scream that I was the newspaper delivery man, not a thief, before this dangerous sceptic decided to call off her savage animals. It had been almost two years since I'd delivered her paper, always at the same time of day, and she had no idea. I didn't exist. People like me, she'd never seen them up close before, if only through her black sunglasses combined with the tinted windows of her expensive car.

Normally, I threw the copies over the fence onto the lawn. I never would have dared to venture any further. Besides, there wasn't any other way. I don't know what had gotten into me that morning, one of her heavily armed bodyguards insisted I enter, I said 'No way, not possible, it's not in my contract.'

'We're only asking you to go put the newspaper down over there,' he insisted. Fucking hell!

It wasn't until afterward that I understood the son of a bitch had played me, just to see me be devoured by the guard dogs. 'Good Lord!' screamed the light-skinned woman in her floral robe, 'What is that?' and the dogs immediately obeyed her index finger pointed towards the aberrant figure. I shot like a star beneath the other armed dogs' bursts of laughter.

There was also this man approaching his sixties, always well-dressed—suit, straightened tie, shiny shoes—you would've thought he had an appointment somewhere with a dress code. It was too strange. Who dresses like that to go nowhere? Sometimes I still imagine him in front of his mirror flipping a coin to figure out whether he or his reflection more closely resembles the perfect image of himself. At 8 a.m. every day, in the same accoutrements, he waited for me at the corner of the same street, took his newspaper, paid for it and then left. One morning, he looked at me, like really looked at me for the first time, and threw this my way, 'A newspaper delivery man is a brainless nobody, a hick incapable of taking a risk and predicting the consequences, a dog that is sent off barking.'

Having understood nothing of his spiel, I said, 'What? What are you trying to say, monsieur?' Then he started to say something I didn't understand either.

'I'm busy, I have many other deliveries to make.'

'Listen to this, kid, it's much more important than your shitty job.' It was about a Black kid in segregated America who sold magazines, day after day, in order to survive, and it just so happened that these magazines preached the hatred of Black people. But that's not all, the man forced me to follow him. He wanted to show me something. I pulled myself away from his embrace and ran across the street. Because, as far as I know, we weren't in America and the newspaper I delivered preached the hatred of nobody, at least as far as I knew. I turned the question over and over in my head, trying to unravel it in vain, before arriving at the conclusion that I should stop bringing this dude his paper. To be honest, I had the feeling that he wanted to pass me a message, but it was all too vague.

Another time, I was convinced that I had seen the nameless woman from the bus in the same taxi as before. She was wearing the same dress. I was able to make it out in the dead of night. Struck by a sense of rapture, this feeling of witnessing an opportunity that might not come again, I chased after the car, causing nearly half of my deliveries to fall to the ground, but I couldn't catch her. A wheelbarrow with two wooden wheels hit me as it ran into the street, overloaded and out of control— *Watch where you're going, motherfucker, is your head up your ass or something*!

The wheelbarrow man shouted at me by way of apology, then to the pedestrians—*Fucking wheelbarrow! Out of the way!*—all while trying to regain control of his movement, pushing his back against the load with his bare feet on the ground. In the back, his acolyte tried his best to stop it, but this rolling disaster was going to cause a bunch of damage in its wake. And this unfortunate occurrence notwithstanding, seated on the load (huge boxes and sacks tied shut with rope), perched a market woman, a Madan Sara, unbothered, her cell phone at her ear, in the middle of a conversation. I was completely stunned, there was nothing more you could ask for. The taxi disappeared. I spent the rest of the day in a reverie . . .

Stories like these, I could tell tons of them, some are inspired by a malaise, the others are completely absurd.

TWENTY-SEVEN

Driven by a true and irrepressible desire to witness your fall, your failure, long after your brother's visit to the lakou. I hoped to see him come around once more, filled with all the bitterness of your last exchange, invincible and determined to expose the truth about you, your true nature, to push the boundaries by bringing an end to many years of injustice. He would've been our hero, whether we liked it or not. But we never saw him again, the scaredy cat, as though the rest of the world swallowed him whole, from that point on he was stripped of his face, his arms, his legs, his voice, his life force. He never existed, he was nothing more than a fantasy, the fruit of a dream . . . Time does things right. My word, guess who ended up in the hallway one morning, cheery and motivated? The Stranger. Yes, your brother. To get hired, he told us how he convinced the boss that he was the man for the job, that he would deliver this newspaper to all the nooks and crannies of the city and make sure that it was read and discussed in every household.

It was strange to see him after so many years. I didn't let him out of sight. He didn't know who I was. When he came to the lakou, he was too exhausted, too fixated on reuniting with you to notice this little mummified sheep. Me, yup, I noticed him right away. I have to admit, your brother was a little heavy-set, but he had a rare quality in these times where everyone puts on an act, fakes it—he spoke frankly, real blunt. If he was trying to be liked, it was only by the boss. It's understandable. Nobody wants to die in the street delivering the newspaper to some random person. If there's a way of avoiding that, why not? Having the boss in your pocket is like picking up a mountain and squeezing it into a jar, isn't that every working man's dream?

In the beginning, your brother tried everything he could just to get noticed. If someone grabbed a bundle of one hundred papers, he would pick up almost twice as many. He didn't miss a chance to brag about his prowess.

Us: You want to look good, that's it?

Him: I'm just working hard.

Us: You take more than you can deliver in a day and you call that working?

Him: Yeah, if you think I'm going to spend all my life in this hallway, you've got another thing coming. *Pain* translates to *bread* in English. Bread is earned through pain. Some beat themselves up just for a mouthful of food. When the boss learns how skilled I am, he'll give me something else to do. He'll make me into his official car washerman, for example. I'd prefer that to walking up and down the streets with a stack of papers under my arms.

Us: Tell me about it, zanmi nou, you'll stay right where you are, the boss doesn't need anyone here to polish his dipstick or anything else, for that matter. This is the job you've got. If I were you, I'd be trying my best to keep it.

Him: Horseshit!

After about two weeks, he realized that his extra effort led him nowhere. We were all stuck in the same dance. Walking. Delivering. Walking. Dying for a shitty salary (in one year alone, three delivery men were killed by bandits on motorcycles), he changed his tune to make do with what most of us had already given up on: the boss' pennies.

Your brother. Now there's someone who was fearless. Who rose to every challenge. And who took everyone by surprise. Who knows how he managed to cash the cheques made out to the journal. He even had his own clients who paid him cash in hand for deliveries and stated that service was better with him. Soon after, the crazed show-off gave way to a lunatic who sold the boss' goods for his own profit, never mind the consequences. A real hard worker when it was all said and done. Punctual. Disciplined. Not once was he late or absent. He never let a fish off the line. At 5 a.m. sharp, he loaded his stack. Before 7 a.m. he'd already delivered everything. It would be too easy to explain his moral fortitude by the fact that he wanted to impress the boss, making a place for himself though his larceny. The man gave off an obvious desire to outdo himself . . .

TWENTY-EIGHT

'You know that you talk to yourself sometimes,' your bother said, without provocation.

'Is that bad?' I replied, slightly annoyed.

'It's not normal, some may easily think that you're deranged, a lunatic, that you've lost your mind. Plus, you scratch yourself— I don't think you're all there, my man.'

'But I am here,' I objected, 'I'm good.'

'In that case, better to talk to other people, folks call that a conversation.'

His voice reminded me of you when you taught everyone your lessons, you imposed your image of things. Two days after this brief conversation, he approached me again, with a sense of hindsight that we didn't recognize in him, 'Fuck, this job is pretty hard, isn't it?' he judged, 'But try to quit and you'll see how much you'll suffer before you find something else. Even folks who have their diplomas and went to college have a hard time. You've got to pimp yourself out, otherwise you've got no shot. Don't you see how they talk sometimes, the people who have a job, you'd think they survived the apocalypse. With their salaries, it's enough to get things up and running, but that's not the question, on the contrary, it's all thanks to their hard work, but they brag about it too much, I think . . .'

I listened without reacting. The loudest voice is the one that works, that pays the bills, and too often it's the voice of a man. But I couldn't see where he was coming from, nor how to get him to talk about you, about the essential. He still didn't know who I was . . .

'Anyway, you, worked here for long?'

'Long enough, yeah.'

'Got any family?'

'Nope, and you?'

'Oh, a few honeys, five kids and an asshole of a brother.' He emphasized these words. An ASSHOLE of a brother!

Things were hopping in the hallway. The newspaper would soon be ready. The machine room greeted us with the final noises of its labour. We got ready to head out, everyone with their stack of papers. I had to learn more about this brother. It was now or never. So, I cast my line. 'I'm sorry, I don't mean to be nosy, but I get the impression you don't carry him in your heart, this brother you mentioned before, one might think that you really despise the man.'

'That's pretty much it.' he confirmed. 'He can burn in hell, the motherfucker betrayed me, it's a long story.'

I encouraged him to keep talking. 'I'm not here to chitchat and we don't have all day, there are only a few minutes left before roll-out, but I'm quite interested to know if folks are as evil as they say, as long as it's all the same to you.'

And, goddamn, to my great satisfaction he began spewing all his resentment—

'He was mean, but he was mostly a coward who fled so far away from his responsibilities that they didn't matter any more, they disappeared forever. It's no surprise. He always tended to gravitate towards his own desire, reinforcing it any way possible, leaving the rest behind, even in the harshest adversity. I wasn't that naive, he was my brother, and I loved him. But I would've thought about myself, too, and all the other scenarios. At first, our thing wasn't too risky. We sold weed. It saved our butts on rainy days. We smoked some, too. Things were turning out pretty good, until the day he brought a piece home, to shift things into a higher gear, as he put it. I had never seen one before. At the same time astonished and with an air of hesitation, I took it from his hands and turned it around in all directions. I'll admit that it was a beautiful object. But it's a bad idea, I said, we can't, it can only end badly. He knew how to convince me. He always managed, no matter how strong my arguments, to put a feeling of his before my eyes, and put his own words into my mouth, and there was nothing I could do to shake it. Go ahead, one big job and it'll be the last, he promised. No more slaving away, selling grass just to survive. In truth, what does that get us?

Nothing. A life with everything we need, don't you dream about that? Do you always want to come in behind just to gather the crumbs? Haven't you been through enough? What are you waiting for? Some benevolent God to come down to earth with a bag of money just for you, or are you waiting to die?

'Money and luxury, they were always an obsession for him. But he wasn't entirely wrong. Our disappointment had been growing for a while. So, I breathed deep and asked him, What's the plan? He'd already picked out a house to rob, studied the comings and goings of the owner, a businessman who wouldn't be home that night. The asshole even claimed to know how he would put the dogs out of commission who were standing guard around the house. Deactivate the alarm, etc. All I had to do was watch our asses.

'In his words, it was simple. The day of the job, a little after midnight, he placed a ladder against the gate of the target house, then he gave me the sign to climb over and point out the location of the dogs in the yard. What a terrible idea! I thought in the back of my mind, but there was no chance of him listening to me. What are you talking about? Climb over the gate. A window or some other kind of secret opening would be smarter, but this right here, we'll be caught, ripped to shreds and scooped up with a tiny spoon. We won't even have a chance to look our killers in the face so that our ghosts can haunt them for the rest of their lives. Shut up! You're not the one who gets to decide, do as I say, if my plan fails because of you, I'll kill you myself. He stuck to his guns. With a weight in the pit of my stomach, I sprang into action, did a sweep of the yard and didn't see any dogs, maybe they . . . Impossible, interrupting me, these monsters are trained not to sleep at night, they're soldiers, sentinels, are you sure there's nothing that moves? I wasn't sure. In the darkness, the house and everything around it looked like a scene from a horror film. But I couldn't let my brother know that I was scared to death, that if I could, I would've given anything not to be where I was. By the same token, I was the only one he could trust. I climbed back down the ladder, because now I had to create a diversion to draw the guard dogs away, at which time he would climb through the gate. Barely had I approached the fence, with too much haste, when I realized that the dogs had become agitated and started to growl—a whole regiment gathered in the shadows. Then it was the alarm's turn, sirens loud enough to wake the dead. The beasts became enraged. All the lights in the house came on. A man in a robe burst from the house with a rifle. He hurtled down the front steps, followed by the dogs, my brother rushed towards the ladder. The man pointed his gun in the direction of the fleeting shadow.

'My brother took himself for a real thief, a professional, a virtuoso. But in reality, he had no clue what he was doing, compared to these dudes who can empty a house for you in no time at all with the occupants sleeping in the other room, unnoticed, clean. In a hurry to get himself caught, the moron had forgotten to bring the pistol. Then, to ward off danger, I fired a couple rounds. Fuck, you killed him! cried my brother. What was I supposed to do? Either I take things into my own hands, or my brother's done for. What we needed was a better plan. Thinking back on it, it wasn't so much the way things played out that bothered him, but realizing that his brother had grown up and was capable of things he couldn't imagine, that was it. We're fucked! he shouted. How are we fucked? Look, he handed me the coat, that's all I could get my hands on before the alarm went off. What can we do with that? We could sell it. To whom? I don't know. Flashing lights. Shit, it's the police! Let's roll out, fast! I didn't get out in time. I landed ten years, while he was off chilling in the woods—I didn't hear a word from him. When I got out of prison, I went looking for him everywhere in vain. The tiny room where we lived was occupied by two other renters. And then I had an idea to take a trip to our parents' village. It's common, fugitives and ex-cons often go hiding in the countryside. That's how I found my brother, seated in a rocking chair in the shade of a baobab, dressed like an old African sage, surrounded by a band of hicks. He greeted me as if I were a stranger. I had to watch my step. My presence disturbed him. He didn't want to have any connection with his past, that's for sure . . .'

Jounal la parèy—The newspaper's ready!

TWENTY-NINE

Suddenly, the boss appeared at the end of the hall. A pompous fellow, pink and blue. A cup of coffee in hand. The silence that quickly accumulated was deep and glacial, at once worrisome and oddly impressive.

'You think we should applaud him?' whispered Enlightened Colleague to me, extracting a muffled laugh.

As he moved forward, the hallway seemed longer and longer. Like the bursts of joy from the neighbourhood when the electricity is restored, the thought detonated in my mind—our petty grifts would be unveiled sooner or later, and I, too, was culpable. I started freaking out. 'You've been a real idiot,' I cursed myself, 'you should've been happy with your rotten salary, now look what'll happen: the boss'll fire you, you won't be able to pay your rent or feed yourself, you ruined everything. You're chilling in your corner. You weren't paying attention to the guys, they still want to hurt you, if they realize that you're trying to drop a dime on them, it's over for you, they'll send you straight to hell . . .'

The boss stopped dead, turned towards me (my heart nearly gave out), then towards your brother. Moron! You might know how to run, but you don't know how to hide. Then, with a nearly spontaneous gesture, like an actor, or closer to a king addressing his subjects, he spun around to make sure to capture the attention of his audience. 'The man you see here is a dirty thief, a cheat, and because of this, he's fired.' Just like you, your brother didn't give the slightest indication of fear or shame. 'If there are other crooks among you who wish to try,' the boss continued, 'be aware that next time the culprit will end up in the grave, and I'll personally make sure that he stays there.'

When the evening came, I thought about it once more. Life's a bitch. The law of the strongest never ceasing to prevail. It was a hard day, I was exhausted, and I fell right asleep. I dreamt that the boss threatened to shoot me in the head if I didn't rat out everyone who was stealing his precious pennies. Meanwhile, my Enlightened Colleague—although he didn't have the same face, his voice an echo in the void—gave a speech on the eminent death of the delivery profession. 'Oh yes, monsieur, it's obvious, with computers, androids, touch-screen tables and other high-tech thingamajigs. It's difficult. The good old delivery man is what we might call an extraterrestrial, a dunce who doesn't understand the function of time amid all these gadgets and this madcap race towards the digital.' All of a sudden, it seemed to me that this big slug of a boss no longer wanted to make me out for a cockroach, a scandal. As though awakened from an old torpor, now in the grips of an illuminating vision, his logorrhoea filled the space, 'Our duty is to adapt to the caprices of our audience,' he put forth with an air of conviction, overconfident, 'to follow the pace of time. Paper or digital, who cares. The goal is to rake in the money . . .'

A month after the scene in the hallway, I came across your brother in the street, but he didn't notice me. He was hardly recognizable, in rags, exhausted, wasting away before my very eyes. His scraps of clothing gave off a fetid odour. A cadaver in search of a place to lie in peaceful repose. I didn't think it was possible for him to fall this low. His dismissal was apparently not the worst thing that had happened to him.

THIRTY

The memory of the random woman from the bus never left me, she was a beautiful mistake. To tell you the truth, I was obsessed. I had so hoped to run into her in the street some day—nowhere in particular—like your brother. Or, maybe I thought someone would start telling me more and more about her, even if it meant unravelling the mystery, causing her to emerge from obscurity and fall in love with someone else. My solitude being what it was—a bottomless pit, a suspended death sentence—I could've pounded the pavement. Returned to the street where the taxi picked her up. Found the taxi. The woman with the book, could you please tell me where you dropped her off? The name of the street? That house she went into, what does it look like? Could you take me there? Here, here's all the money I have. I could've tried to forget her and found consolation elsewhere. How do I explain my state of mind? A part of me (the largest part) needed her and the other was full of doubt. What's the point? Why would she want to see some random guy? I was even trying to convince myself that our encounter had actually happened, that it wasn't a vision, a fantasy that had gotten the best of reality. That I wasn't stuck in one of those stories about zonbi, creatures caught between worlds, forced to do a sorcerer's bidding. A woman as beautiful as a siren invites a man into her imposing and luxurious mansion where a dozen valets are running all over the place, distinguished, upright and methodical. After a sumptuous dinner, the dinner guest and the woman make love all night long. The next morning at dawn, the man wakes up in a cemetery, his head pressed against a tomb, indicating that he only has twenty-four hours left to live . . .

For all these years, I thought about her with such intensity that sometimes my head ached. The problem was this: I had never managed to love another woman. In a way, I was screwed because I mostly frequented prostitutes. But my pay only allowed me this sort of mayhem once every four months. No doubt, the only way out of it was masturbation. And that would eventually turn into a necessary habit. Before going to bed, after waking up—I never went more than twenty-four hours without jerking off, and to top it all off, I was drinking a lot. Sometimes, halfway through, I thought I could see her in front of me, in a skimpy outfit, enticing. Bathed in a soft light, perfectly waxed, she stripped masterfully from head to toe, playing with her G-string, the little slut. She was so real. She invited me to join in, to touch her. I caressed her with one hand while I beat my dick wildly. Oh fuck! Fuck! I was so hard for her. It was real. It was perfect. I really believed it was happening, I believed so hard that heaven was within arm's reach when, all of a sudden, the light went out. Everything came tumbling down after I blew my load, letting loose a pathetic moan—uuuunnnnhhhh! And then I started to believe once more that I would never see her again.

THIRTY-ONE

So, why am I expecting the police? Let's look at the facts, once and for all.

About a month ago, my boss—may the son of a bitch burn in hell—called me from the end of the hallway, 'Hey you, come here,' handed me a piece of paper, and dryly said, 'Starting tomorrow and for the rest of the month, I want you to deliver to this address first,' and that was it.

'Oh la la,' my Enlightened Colleague said after reading what was written on the piece of paper, 17 Finitude Street, explaining the route to the address. 'This smells fishy, are you sure you're up for it?'

'Well yeah, it's nothing more than a delivery, it'll be fine.'

'OK.' His *OK* sounded more like, *fine, go ahead but don't come back crying later.*

Having been the victim of our boss' perversity, I knew that my Enlightened Colleague hated him. That, for him, I would be advised to tear this piece of paper up and forget about this order. Yes, but not really. I didn't have a choice. You don't tell your boss that you can't do the job you're being paid for. I like my

Enlightened Colleague. He's someone who knows what he wants. But at the time, I defended my choice, perhaps I was incapable of reconciling his point of view with my completely legitimate and absolute sense of duty that tied me to my superior. I regretted my conformism.

First thing next morning, I showed up at the address in question. A house made of lace, hanging like a picture on the flat blue surface of the sky, partially hidden between the trees, its terrace decorated with blue, yellow, red and pink flowers, with wide and tall doors and windows. The wrought-iron sliding gate was open. A little gravel path led to an entrance where there were no gorillas or snarling dogs. Cush cush, squeaked the gravel beneath my feet. My bundle of newspapers under my arm. Why did the boss send me here? I asked myself. What piqued my curiosity even more was to learn who lived in this house that needed to be taken care of first thing, and why exactly had the boss chosen me, and not someone else, for this mission. In the end, I told myself these questions didn't matter—do your job, and beat it.

I didn't anticipate what would happen next.

As I've briefly mentioned, my encounters with certain clients have left me scarred. For the most part, they're something beyond rejection, verging on humiliation. The memories are still alive, so I had every interest in respecting my limits. The intimacy of a subscriber is sacred, you're not supposed to encroach upon it. That's just one of the many constraints that seemed completely logical to me. But suddenly my Enlightened Colleague's conclusion came to mind. How could I be satisfied by simply leaving the newspaper on the front steps and continuing on my way like there was nothing intriguing or odd about this situation? I rang the doorbell. It was the only way of finding out who this special person the boss had put at the front of the list was. A voice called from the terrace: 'Bonjour.' I looked up.

It was her. The nameless woman from the bus. Standing there, a steamy mug in hand.

'It's you!' she shouted straightaway. 'What are you doing here?' Good God! She remembered me. 'The young man from the bus!' A few years had passed since. But it was as if, from the moment she stepped into that taxi that day downtown, nothing in the world had changed.

My eyes bugged out in shock, 'Ye-ye-yes,' I stammered, 'that's me, I have your newspaper.' I put it down in front of the door and ran off.

I couldn't believe what had just happened, nor could I continue my deliveries. I headed home right after, assaulted by a barrage of questions along the way, each one more acute and fuzzy than the last. Seeing her again was so unexpected and devastating. I spent the rest of the day under the influence of strange feelings. And at night, I tossed and turned in bed. Trying to fix my attention on something else, an elusive thought, only amplified its stagnation. If I could, I would have kept the whole world at bay for longer. The whole night. A whole lifetime. For nothing less than to escape from this black hole, this internal disturbance. To return to the time where I could dream only of her, to follow the illusion of getting to know her and a deep desire for more, which was nothing other than the cosmic vertigo of the senses. Yes, I loved her. A little more every day, every week, every month and every year that passed. On the other hand, I was afraid that my feelings for her were like some kind of raft on which my loneliness would be set adrift to avoid being swallowed by the swelling void of her existence and disappear. Now that I wasn't really sure of anything any more, let's just say that I didn't want to fuck it all up. I didn't know where to begin because, like I said before, the world hadn't changed. Whatever I do or say, everything had stayed the same as it was that day downtown. Meanwhile, her taxi disappeared around the corner. As far as the newspaper is concerned, I could have arranged things so that I didn't have to deliver it to her house. I told myself that it was too soon to see her again, especially since I still hadn't found anything to say to her. But I wouldn't have wanted her to go and check in with the decrepit receptionists. *I find your delivery man very strange.* And for this information to make it all the way to the boss.

My head was imploding.

I wasn't at all tempted to report this episode to my Enlightened Colleague. I had already witnessed him launch into a long tirade regarding the tacit associations of chance, while on the other hand maintaining that accidents do not exist, that everything is predetermined by a force that our spiritual poverty prevents us from comprehending. 'Oh, monsieur, how many times must I repeat it? The boss is a sly one, a snake, a dog who calls his mistresses fat cows . . .' I didn't want to waste my time. I also had to stop myself believing that he had an answer for everything.

THIRTY-TWO

The next morning, the woman invited me inside in the most nonchalant way possible, 'Well, come on in, don't stand outside!' A sweet injunction. I didn't ask for as much. But I thought to myself, you're a delivery man, you have no right to be standing where you are, you don't want any trouble.

Listen, the Other Within appeared to say, you're not going to disappoint this fairy princess, are you, and besides, it's not like she's some kind of ordinary subscriber, you've already met before, right? OK, fine!

I went in, shamefully reminded of how, on the bus, I'd allowed my gaze to subtly dance from the emergence of her breasts to her legs, consumed by these bestial urges that would have overcome any man. All obsessive love begins this way, more or less. I also recalled that she had no luck with men. They're all manipulators with power . . .

The house was tastefully decorated. The light shining through the bay of windows accentuated its charm. I'd never seen such a welcoming home before. The feeling that I didn't belong never left me. But she asked for me to come in. She must have been interested in me; she must have been in love with me.

The events that followed vindicated my dreams. A second after, she threw herself at me. On the couch. On the bed. Against the sink in the kitchen. On the dining-room table . . . She was exactly the way she was in my masturbatory hallucinations. I was living an unexpected dream. Heaven and Earth could have disappeared, and I wouldn't have noticed.

I must admit that I wasn't always very engaging or effective with the ladies. The reason must be because in the lakou, according to the code of conduct the Emperor imposed, girls and boys were separated from one another. You ordered the girls to play with other girls and do girly things. The boys played with other boys and did manly things. I grew up believing that women and men were destined to live in two different worlds. I can count on one hand the sexual experiences I've had. Two female students at the School of Ethnology on a 'pedagogical outing'. A White Westerner, I'll never forget her, ha ha ha! She told me to fuck her like I beat the drum at the moment when the lwa enter the perestil. And this one night when I met the pastor's daughter from the Christian Church of the Tabernacle of Grace, guided by the creaking of your bed and the mooing of your milk cows. A funny story, really. Two days later, chance had brought us face to face, she and I, halfway between our neighbouring and enemy territories. At the end of our brief conversation, she told me where she often went to watch the stars, the fairies of infinity, laying on the ground, facing the sky in the middle of what resembled a tiny thicket. She loved these moments of solitude, completely free from the family hearth where nothing else existed beyond the omnipotence of a singular moral, that of the *living God*, and only those who resembled her, shared her certainties, her virtues, were her brothers and sisters.

I will not mention those for whom one god is not enough, the folks who go to church by day and twist and turn around the potomitan by night.

If my memory serves me right, these radical Protestants, capable of the worst in the name of their God, came to the lakou once or twice to preach to us *the Good News of the Gospel of Christ's Rebirth* with their Bible verses and apotropaic prayers. We tried to tell them how Vodou advocates for unity beyond beliefs, welcomes everyone, regardless of their walk of life, their origins, the colour of their skin. But they were not there to be welcomed. They wanted to impose their own beliefs and rituals upon us. You threw them and their pillow of a Bible out with fury. Afterwards, they threatened to set fire to the badji. It was serious. Their message was absolute. The authority comes from the Highest. He who resists shall perish. No village, no country can evolve outside of the progress of the Gospel, people run astray in favour of vain observances, barked the monotheists. This was far from an isolated attitude. In many regions of the country, the Vodouphobic machine cracked the whip, largely supported by White missionaries in cooperation with the local authorities, in hopes of abolishing this *diabolic religion* and civilizing Haiti once and for all. The disastrous impact of this operation remains unclear for the time being. The whole quarrel between *good* and *evil*, the *best* and the *worst* made no sense to me. All gods are the same: passive and speechless. According to my Enlightened Colleague, the dispute dates back to the dolorous and obscene era of our colonized ancestors, where only God—White and Western, the same as yesterday, today and forever—judged, as the arbitrator of peoples, which nations had the right to exist. Waging war and killing in the name of this God was common currency. The authors of these crimes had motivations that were as hare-brained as they were unfathomable. The Holy Bible was their compass and guide from which each of them tore out the slice of truth that suited them, according to their understanding and fixed goal.

How is religious morality really created?

The answer is simple, my Enlightened Colleague explained once more, over time and with a show of strength, the pastor or the spiritual guide applies pressure to the ignorance and conscience of his devotees. First, gentle tremors occur, provoked by aversion, a nascent distrust for a specific, vilified other. Then comes an absurd rancour that develops over time, intensifying, turning into the immense wheels of hatred. All of you, you and your sheep and your counterfeit gods, must carry your own cross down the same path as Christ or you will wind up in every inferno imaginable. Because it was you, cursed souls, fervent admirers of the devil, with your filthy customs, your vices, who were responsible for all the ills of the world. No matter how overwhelmed I was by your hypocrisy, it didn't hold a candle to their biblical horseshit. It was obvious to these charred minds that the pastor's daughter was one of Christ's little lambs, the daughter of a respectable family, born at God's breast, brought up to respect the morals of the Gospel—that is, with respect for the absolute truth and salvation extolled by their ministry which she could not deny. But that wasn't the case at all, in fact. She was totally aware of the kind of world she wanted to live in, and the kind of life she wanted to have. In their eyes, I was an undesirable type of guy. In their neck of the woods, there was no place for fraternizing with non-believers, a Vodou drummer to boot. Death to the Golden Calf! Each donkey must be left to graze in its own pasture. Let's say there's place for two donkeys in the same pasture. Paradise–Hell. Christian–Vodouizan. God–Satan. Day–Night. Truth–Lies. To these God-fearing fools, it was unforgiveable that one could even consider any of these combinations. Syncretism my ass! Inviting God, the Creator of heaven and Earth to dine at the same table as the Vodou Spirits, have you lost your damn mind?!

In this cool and starry November night, the pastor's daughter snuggled into the arms of the young sinner. The scene was memorable. But with the nameless woman from the bus, it was something else altogether.

THIRTY-THREE

What prison, what punishments could take away my images of her? In the kitchen, pouring herself another tea, before coming back to bed or the couch next to me, or seated in a robe on her stool in front of the vanity. Her naked reflection, a completely casual sensuality, aloof, without pretence, her tender flower, her generous breasts, her soft, wavy black hair. In the cerulean blue around her eyes oscillated a sweet sadness. The way she delicately placed her teacup onto its saucer to answer the phone that rang for the first time since we started seeing each other.

I regret not being able to hear what she said, caught up in a whirlwind of daydreams. We didn't talk much. When in love, it seems to me that there's not much to say, each word is an offence to the expressive majesty of a simple glance. I gazed at her with such intensity that I could no longer feel my body, my heart beating or my own breath. It was at once an atrocious and marvellous sensation, the beginning of an uncontrollable fragility, the kind that alienates, eating away at us. Most of the time, when something sublime happens to us with another person, you convince yourself that it will continue, never coming to an end. You become self-centred, looking to control everything to guarantee complete and utter exclusivity with this person whose true intentions are difficult to read. Love involves absence, abandonment, rejection in its most brutal, most absolute forms. It can reach incredibly inhumane proportions.

In the time our story lasted, seven mornings, and even after, I was incapable of imagining her being with anyone else but me. How could she go this far without being in love with me? Is a woman capable of loving several men the same way, with the same fervour? Persuaded of having experienced something exceptional with her, something you don't just give up, I constantly repeated to myself—No, it wasn't phantasmagoric, nor was it a personal obsession, a source of dread, a projection. To her I was not some pedestrian, an ordinary man who could have been, like anyone else, a means of filling a void. Because she's not the kind of woman who wants to hear her robe is pretty, and that's it, nothing more, nothing less. Nor is she the kind of woman who is ready to put her whole life on hold to run off with you to the end of the earth, not knowing the difference between what her gut and her hormones are telling her and her true feelings. She also had a bunch of other qualities that I deliberately attribute to her and that, to me, constitute the essence of a real woman's personality. I loved her to the point that it was impossible to imagine it couldn't be reciprocal. I was losing my mind.

'So, what's your name after all?'

How was it possible, four mornings later, that I still had not told her my name, nor had I looked to find out hers?

By way of response, I began caressing her back, the tips of her breasts, between her legs . . . She bent her head to the side, raising her hips slightly, an umpteenth spark came over us.

Like the astrological sign we're born into, a name is a fiction, I later thought, realizing that I had still never managed to learn anyone's name, not a single one on planet Earth. At the paper, we limited ourselves to *colleague*. All right, colleague, we're off! Have nice day, colleague! Take care of yourself, colleague! Before her, nobody had ever thought to ask me what my name was.

I still wasn't sure how to respond to her question. She could have misinterpreted my silence. Or worse, she could have judged me from the start. It's true, some women would prefer to burn in hell than to have a relationship with a newspaper delivery man, a dirtbag, a bore, a bum, a loser and other nasty things they scream at the top of their lungs to keep their distance from guys like me. Anyhow, you're better off sleeping with a woman who's paid for that sort of thing . . .

'Tell me your name,' she insisted, 'You know, I've been with jerks and jealous types who watched me every step I took, made my life impossible to live, all because of one or two nights. But you, you seem kind, even if I have a little trouble explaining to myself what is going on. We met on a bus by complete chance, and a few years later you're here, in my house, and we still don't know each other's names. At the same time, there's not much more to say, it's time passing by . . .' She contemplated for a moment, looking me deep in the eyes, and decided: 'I'm going to call you P, my lucky letter.'

THIRTY-FOUR

The seventh and final day of our adventure, after particularly intense sex when she asked me to tie her up, put it in her ass, smack her harder, you know, completely dominate her. I think she wanted to explore something different with me, or at least to show me this side of her sexuality. It was, how can I put it? I don't know. I just had to filter her out—*Yes*! *Fuck me, damn it*! *That's it, I'm gonna come*!—to really feel like I was preying on a defenceless soul, punishing her, violating her. For a second, I had the terrible thought—*I love her too much, she cannot continue to exist*—to break her neck and be done with her. It was so sudden and hard to resist. I had to drown out this insanity before it was too late, I closed my eyes, quickened my pelvic thrusts, concentrating on the pleasure the nameless woman took from it. *Uuuunnnnhhhh*!

I wondered afterwards if I should have followed through with that thought, eliminating her.

Then, as I was laying on the bed next to her, I had the sudden feeling of being watched, like some hidden camera was filming us from the beginning. I tried to reason with myself—calm down, you're tired, it's been an intense couple of days, this encounter completely changed your life. But I remained convinced that it was true. It occupied so much space in my mind that it only left room for one thought—get the hell out of there, fast. I jumped out of bed, threw on my clothes, grabbed my bundle of newspapers (which I chucked into a sewer drain on the way home) and took off running. My attitude was disconcerting. 'What's gotten into you?' she asked. I didn't dare tell her about it. She would have found it ridiculous. 'What?! Ha ha ha, a hidden camera!' Dumbstruck, I recalled the way my Enlightened Colleague had described this delivery—*it smells fishy*. And the boss is a *huge pervert*. If there was a hidden camera, who installed it? Was one of her past lovers struggling to come to grips with their separation, trying to annoy her for kicks? The boss didn't send me to fuck one of his mistresses or his wife solely to trick me, to trick me, to trick me, to trick me, to trick me . . .

Caught in a flurry of mishandled emotions, my mind came unhinged. I ruminated over the story for the rest of the day and night. It churned violently, like a tornado. It was like I had been cursed by an evil spell, the fury of a Vodou god. The feeling completely consumed me. It's terrible to imagine you've done something wrong without the means of understanding what or how to fix it. I thought I was going nuts. Not only because of the feeling that I was being filmed with this woman, but especially because I was afraid that the boss was really behind everything, pulling the strings, intent on humiliating and manipulating me like my Enlightened Colleague, like everyone who has had the misfortune of being one of his subordinates. My brain like mush,

I paced back and forth around the room, in every direction, till the end of the night, searching, in vain, for a clear answer. Nothing could calm the extreme anxiety I felt. Was I facing the apocalypse, or had the pernicious bifurcation of my conscience thrust me into a dead end? To this day, I can't tell if I was acting under the influence of my lone troubles or if I was responding to a real threat of danger. All that I knew was that I wouldn't be able to survive for long in such a mental state. I went back to her house the next day before sunrise.

THIRTY-FIVE

No matter how deeply you wish for it, you can't make up for lost time. Every morning for a week, at the same time, I delivered the newspaper in hopes of seeing her again. But the nameless woman from the bus was no longer there. The gate remained closed with a lock and chain. The house looked empty. I guess she went on vacation, to the countryside or somewhere else. If that were the case, she would be back, and I could explain to her why I scurried away like that the last time. If she was dead in the house, we'd know about it soon. A dead body starts to reek after a few days.

One dawn followed the next, and the situation continued, unchanged. The house remained abandoned. Thoughts kept pulling at me. Some thoughts led to other more far-fetched ones. *No, no, no. Fuck*! I shouted, imagining something even more terrible. Sleeping with a zonbi. She wasn't a zonbi, nor a hallucination. She wasn't walking slowly, with her head facing down. She didn't have a nasal voice. Besides, zonbi wander around at night. My mind was in chaos. I couldn't bear the possibility of her disappearance. Thinking about it filled me with the unfamiliar feeling of having lost the best part of myself. The feeling continued to grow as I hurled the newspaper over the cursed gate, in compliance with the boss' command, because no order to the contrary had been issued. We deliver the newspaper with or without the client present. I lingered to admire this house where she and I had lived the most beautiful, striking beginning of a love story. Certain nights, I drank myself into a stupor, beating my dick ragged while I imagined the contours of her face, her body, her quivering, her cries of ecstasy. I was hopeless. We're never prepared to deal with loss, to formulate a credible explanation for an absence. I forced myself to accept that it was just one of those things that can happen in life, but I couldn't. No, no, it's not possible. Fuck! Fuck!

Anyway, if I was going to decipher the enigma of her dis-appearance—if I was incapable of turning the page, acting as if nothing had happened—I would have to regain my spirits. And by culling through my memories in search of a word, a gesture, a packed bag, something that could be the source of her departure, I realized that I didn't know her, this woman, at all. She was nameless. I knew absolutely nothing about her—her history, her family, her friends. On the dresser in her room, there was a framed picture. A picture of another woman. On the woman's face, there was an expression of satisfaction so great that it couldn't be anything more than one of those clichéd stock photos sold with the frame—there to fill a void, to offer a simulation.

Walking past it, hold on, I wondered what I looked like. It's funny, I've never seen my face before, nor have I ever attempted to see my reflection. I remember, in the throes of our second morning of passion, she told me while kissing that she loved my lips, that they were generous and soft. But nothing about my eyes, my cheeks, my nose, my chin, my eyebrows, my hair, my ears. How much does our face say about us? Would mine be a sort of agreement, a precarious balance between my wrinkles? Would it be the opposite, ironic, the foundation of the person in the photo? To find out, I would have to look at myself in the piece of mirror hanging on the wall, without lowering or hiding my face in my hands when I walk past. What's certain is that it's not possible I resemble the person I am inside. When you're in tune with yourself, that's all you need to protect yourself from the turmoil of the world. 'But that's not enough,' the Other Within erupted, 'We rely on the smallest particle of infinity. Everyone's face is a simplification of the self, a hypothesis, a facade, a fragile spring, an open grave, get back to it, keep thinking about this woman . . .' Even more questions emerged: what does this Other Within know that I don't already? Or, that I should know? Does it matter? What about this story concerns him?

THIRTY-SIX

The Other Within and I admit, it's a strange thing. When someone disappears it's like they were hidden, trapped, erased by the shadows. As though they were screaming, gesticulating, doing everything possible for someone to realize that they're there, still breathing. We sometimes feel as if we can smell them, breathing the uncertain haze of their being; but it's impossible to see them, to hear them. And as time goes by, they cease to be hidden, trapped, erased by the shadows and they become shadows—absence—themselves . . .

If a person declared dead doesn't respond when you call into the govi, it means that they're not really there, the Very Old Sheep explained to me, they're out there, somewhere in nature, or tied to the bòkò's post, waiting to be reduced to slavery, or to be turned into a goat . . .

The govi, the fà, or whatever other so-called portal to the horizon, the afterlife, everything else seemed like complete nonsense to me. A joke that wasn't funny at all. If the gods existed, wouldn't they be the first to know? Would they leave a motherfucker like you to decide in their stead? Unless they were only useful unto themselves or called to be instruments of mankind.

My luck had always been my lack of faith, sometimes even in the nature and plasticity of the trances of this heart in my chest . . .

While the world kept turning like before, this woman was no longer there, she was probably in grave danger.

In truth, I wasn't ready to throw myself into this absurd adventure which amounted to a search for a missing person. And beyond that, I wasn't even sure that there was a disappearance. Should someone be held to count? Apart from the phone call (she had hung up a little abruptly) that I thought about later, when this story about the hidden camera started taking up too much space in my head, there was nothing that I could consider abnormal.

THIRTY-SEVEN

It rained a lot in May and at the beginning of June, like nearly every year, before the sun beats down on the earth in summer. This room turns into an oven, making it impossible to sleep, day or night, cooling off a little before dawn, only to start heating up again at nine or ten o'clock in the morning.

After a night spent fighting off mosquitos and sleeplessness, my dead-end thoughts, I reluctantly found myself in the hallway, exhausted, awaiting the newspaper that I had no desire to deliver. Suddenly, the Other Within startled me, saying, 'Here's our guy.' The boss had just entered the hallway for the first time since your brother's dismissal. Who's turn was it to get fired? Oddly, as though trying not to be noticed, my Enlightened Colleague grabbed a newspaper, held it in front of his face and began to vaguely flip through its pages. His fingers trembled. He put the newspaper back down. Then, picked it back up. It was so obvious that he was panicking. I'd never seen him like that before.

You could hear the seconds go by, they were so loud and intense, as the big fat beast appeared, blue and pink, human abjection in its most indelibly striking form.

'He's the one!' screamed the Other Within, as though he had just been awakened.

'He's what?'

'The one responsible for the disappearance of your little girl-friend.' He'd just strengthened an idea I'd already been working on. I could've disregarded it, ignoring him, but the Other Within has never lied to me before, ever. Upon my arrival in the lakou, he told me straightaway, 'Watch out for the Emperor, he's a dirty liar, an impostor. Mark my words, the boss is the one who orchestrated the whole thing, he's a scoundrel, how many times has your Enlightened Colleague told you so? Who else could it be? Open your eyes. He gave you the address and the delivery order. He tricked you. He's been seeing this woman for a while, just one in a pile of mistresses. To him, mistresses are prettier, sweeter, more talented, more everlasting than wives who, as soon as they cross the threshold of the nuptial gates in the arms of an imbecile, begin to wither and wither and wither, until they die. Mistresses always show the same passion. They're where the journey begins. A married man without mistresses is a branch that sulks in the forest.' It was the Other Within that was still talking to me, but it felt like a rejoinder from the Very Old Sheep, with the residue of personal experience. 'Truth be told, it's not about mistresses or lovers, but about being yourself, about freely wanting what you please. Freedom enflames desire, the inalienable gift from the self to the other, and this gift called desire is composed of the depths of the heavens and the tiniest morsal of humanity.'

'The boss loved this woman, even though he wished he didn't. She loved him, too, at least he had the audacity to think so. The idea of her vanishing, or that she might be dead, had always been more bearable than starting a family with her. Simply put, he cultivated passion without living it, either that or he lived it only in part. Regardless, it wasn't enough for him to relinquish that which allowed him to retain his status, of being a boss and the father to a respectable family. He was fully aware that he was playing a dangerous game, that his petty addictions would reveal themselves. But it was impossible for him to do otherwise, namely, not loving his mistresses and guarding himself from his feelings, his mental contradictions. As he wandered from one psychological extreme to another, this almost vital need he had to torture others, to take pleasure in their suffering, intensified and gave root to the idea of manipulating you, trapping you. Your experience with the Emperor taught you a lot about men. The way they operate. Their vain passions. They're capable of all kinds of ugliness! And they're united, each in their own way, in their delusions. The boss has a bit of the Emperor in him, and vice versa. One is just like the other, and they both share small pieces of one another. They're all Emperors, bosses, destroyers of dreams, abominations. We should eliminate them all, yes, all of them.'

The Other Within seemed more invasive, dark and intransigent than he had ever been since he revealed himself to me as a child. His uncontrollable breathing filled the smallest parts of my body and mind. When I closed my eyes, I could almost see the contours of his silhouette forming, decomposing and reforming again in a patchwork of vibrant, fleeting colours, a fulcrum between reverie and reality, between time and its illusions. It was as though I were slipping into the void, completely dispossessed of my being.

What kind of relationship should we have with the Other Within so that he doesn't hold us at his mercy? Is he acting alone? How many of them, hidden in the bushes of the unconscious, are there claiming the right to control us? Are we his fictional invention? Some forest populated by strange beings? Does he originate from a certain abandonment, a mismanagement of the self, our incapacity to take care of ourselves? Is he a spell, an aftershock, an indefatigable god acting out of forgetfulness? Is he a shadow controlling our minds? A discrepancy between our free will and our actions? Is the world a top left spinning by an unknowable force?

We remained frozen in the hallway, the sheep of the factory, awaiting the boss' permission. My Enlightened Colleague guessed right. 'You, you're fired! Go on, beat it' shouted the boss, right in his face.

THIRTY-EIGHT

A scream woke me in the middle of the night. The scream of a woman being chased. *Help me, mezanmi, tanpri*! *Oh my god, please*! Who is going to climb out of bed to help a whore? On the contrary, the mood was jubilant. 'Ah, that bitch, she's gonna get her money's worth!' Her crying continued in the street, imploring and tragic. Slowly smothered, like an ember after a slow braise, into oblivion. I saw the incident as a cautionary tale. And what I would do afterwards perfectly translated the mental state I was in. My despair. Proof of a growing anxiety. I leapt from bed, quickly threw on some clothes, bolted to the random lady's house and ran around outside shouting for an hour. 'Is anyone there? It's me, the young man from the bus, the newspaper delivery man, P, your lucky letter!' No one answered. On the way home, I had the strange feeling like I was fighting against some incredible, unimaginable force, suffering from my very own absence, from the impossibility of being whole. I grated myself so hard that I had blood and bits of flesh under my fingernails. But I didn't feel any pain. Captivated to the point of obsession by the images from the last couple of days, by this Kafkaesque hidden camera that I couldn't manage to escape despite my enormous efforts. I wondered, among other things, if it was a manipulation on the part of my boss, or my own delirious interpretation—the mystery remained complete and insurmountable. I had to go see him and explain everything. Depending on how much his face revealed, I would know where I stood, more or less. But, without his blessing, how could I breach the heavenly vault and speak directly to God? How could I reach him? It felt impossible to me.

'Nothing is impossible,' the Other Within erupted once more. I wasn't listening to him. I chickened out. I loved this woman, but she's not there any more. If we come to find out, contrary to what we believe, that the boss isn't involved, this woman is just off somewhere taking advantage of another young man she met on some other bus or, I don't know, passing from one body to the next, spreading herself wide. I had to forget her, pretend like she never existed, but that too felt impossible to me.

I would go see my boss and explain everything to him. What exactly? 'Monsieur, I cannot deliver to the address you asked me to any more, because the woman has been unreachable for going on a month.' Or maybe, 'Monsieur, swear to me that you'll tell the whole truth and nothing but the truth?' Very well. 'A subscriber to your newspaper is believed to be missing, do you know her? For how long? When, where and how did you two meet? Did you ask one of your delivery men to prioritize her delivery? Don't all subscribers deserve to be treated the same way, regardless of their gender, race, skin colour or background? Are there hidden intentions behind such personalized attention? How would you define your relationship to her? Have you ever slept together?'

Finally, I decided to visit my Enlightened Colleague. Everything went over my head. One time, he'd talked to me about a spot on the other side of town where he knocked a few back with his buddies. After what had just happened to him, it was the best thing he could do. I didn't even have the time to wave hello because, as soon as he saw me, he got out of his chair and started to yell. He was thinner and completely wasted. 'What the fuck are you doing here, motherfucker! Don't you have that shitty newspaper to deliver for your dickhead boss!? Oh, I see, the gentleman has also been bitten by the snake who infiltrates everything, crushing, ensnaring everyone around, even his mistresses, to better control them—is that it!?' He was yelling even louder. 'May the sky crash down on top of you, your boss and the rest of the bosses in the world! We don't exist. We've never existed.' His anger was indescribable and infinite. A bolt of lightning in flesh and blood. I'd have loved to encounter once more that man who took his time answering my questions. But I didn't have the right to speak to him any more. No longer present, he was drowning in the belly of this ocean that never spits anything back out. An ocean of despair. 'Beat it, and don't ever come bother me with your bullshit again!' His voice was enveloped in mist. He leant forward, stared intensely at the ground and clenched his fists as though at this very moment he wished he were six feet underground. Then, he burst into tears, 'My mother's very sick, you know, she's losing her mind, she doesn't recognize me any more, she's in so much pain. There's medications I have to buy, and now I'm out of work, I've no way of helping her out. She's going to die, and what'll become of me?' His face was a disaster, soaked with sweat, mucus and tears. My heart broke. I wanted to take him into my arms and tell him how sorry I was, but it was too difficult for me. I left without revealing my reasons for coming. He'd said enough, everything was crystal clear. To the Emperors, the bosses and the jackals, the rest of the world is a meadow full of sheep. Folks who devour their fellow man don't deserve to exist! I shouted these words alone in the street, as though I were speaking to someone. And then, an idea occurred to me that would soon warrant a visit by the police and probably a very long stint in the national penitentiary.

THIRTY-NINE

Noon on the dot. As usual, the heart of the city was white-hot. A magma of noise, the living, all sorts of concoctions. A deafening and prolonged end of the world. Everything was moving so fast, in every direction. Madness, brought on especially by the harshness of living and the incommensurable number of needs, stenches and obstacles. Added to this was a massive protest in which the so-called aggrieved—by the indifference of the state, the insecurity, the poverty, the insalubrious streets, the hunger, and so on—gave the impression that they were there to dance and unwind as much as anything else. They were chomping at the bit, shaking their hips like on a dance floor, chanting the lyrics of popular songs. Believing that their misery was not dramatic at all, that death could go fuck itself, that they felt better living with their feet knee-deep in shit than if it had been another way, otherwise it wouldn't have been a real life at all. Downtown is a failure as far as the eye can see. We have a hard time believing that our political leaders can recognize reality. Thumbing their nose at everything while driving by in their air-conditioned cars. Torsos bare, their shirts tied around their waists, men push and shove in front of trucks full of merchandise, pulling with all their strength heavy packages they carried on their shoulders or on their heads. They split the crowd throwing their hips right to left and left to right. Fine dancers fighting against misery. Women sang to lure in clients, sheltered by wide-brimmed hats or umbrellas to protect themselves from the sun, in the middle of hills of trash more than two centuries old. Indefatigable songstresses of hope. Where did they get the courage?

I had to be patient and adventurous to find these three simple things, without which my plan was impossible: a good suit, a briefcase and a violent, liquid, odourless poison. That'll teach the asshole not to manipulate everyone, I thought to myself, smiling.

One by one, I cut through the bungalows and cluttered pharmacies, carved into the facades on Rue Magasin-de-l'État. Along the sidewalks, immense sawhorses displayed the same items to be found inside the boutiques. Living display cases, grotesque and troublesome. One might say that they'd always been there, and that they'd always be there. When a potential buyer would approach, the merchants would all jump to grab their attention. Each one claimed to have the most authentic, most handsome variety of what I was looking for. A woman grabbed me by the arm and ushered me into a makeshift cabana of undulating sheet metal covered by a tarp, 'Tanpri, myse—please monsieur, buy something from me,' she begged, 'Look, I have everything you need right here: socks, shirts, belts, suit jackets, slacks, ties, perfumes, lotions, deodorants. I haven't sold anything in a week, believe me, a day that starts with a client spells good fortune, men bring me good luck . . .' No sooner had I escaped the market woman's song when another threw a blazer over my shoulders, shoving a briefcase in my hand, 'Here you are, monsieur, they're yours. Come back and pay whenever you'd like, you can find me here no matter what day or what time, I won't budge.' Another vender shot across the street like a bolt of lightning, came back with some other knock-offs, 'A suit, monsieur, cannot be chosen, the suit chooses you, and when it happens, you cannot escape, it's magic. If I can be at your service, try it on, no need to thank me.' I said no thanks, but, say, do you sell any poison that'll kill on the spot? Visibly troubled by my question, he walked back across the street with his rad pèpè without saying another word.

They were all counting on me not returning home empty-handed from this horrid Haitian day, but, sadly, none of their proposals satisfied my taste. I had to look chic, impeccable, and my poison incredibly lethal. Simple things that took me a little while to find, thanks to an old man. Noticing me wander, spinning around in the middle of all these hysterical merchants, he walked up to me and asked in a peaceful voice: 'How can I be of service, my son? Halleluiah!' It didn't look like much, but I left his bungalow a happy man. I had everything I needed to act. The suit, the briefcase and a vial of the most lethal poison you can find on the market these days, to use the old man's words.

I hadn't told anyone about my plan. I couldn't handle the slightest reaction. People might think I was a psychopath—no way, you've lost your mind! You're going to commit a heinous act because a voice in your head told you it was the right thing to do? You need help!

FORTY

I've worked as a delivery man for a while now. I've gathered more knowledge and a wider vision of the city, or what's left of it. I can also say that I've served my country over the years, occasionally taking risks, so people can read their newspaper at home. If they pay for a subscription every month, I told myself, it must be important to them. And I did everything I could to not disappoint them, except under extenuating circumstances, like the days when I was levelled by fatigue and anxiety. Too often we neglect the little things, without which the big things weaken and eventually fall apart.

But I was determined to follow through with my idea. I don't regret a thing, I must admit. I firmly believe that there's something in humans that leads to their fatal downfall. Every second of one's life, every accomplishment, the most impressive to the most banal, carries within it a germ of self-destruction.

The excitement and stress brought on by this moment spirals through my body. There's no way these clothes could be worn by just anybody, I whispered, pulling on this suit that fit me like a dream, lending me the appearance of a big shot, a banker, a business man, a judge, a movie star, somebody light years away from the average paperboy, the poor dog. Sometimes it takes so little for everything to change, to turn things upside down. The whole thing scared me a little bit. All of a sudden, I didn't feel up to it. I was more afraid of missing my shot than getting caught. *Get a hold of yourself, now's not the time!* There was no turning back from this point, even though I was aware that God is unreachable, protected by merciless dogs. Truth be told, the two morons posted at the newspaper's entrance weren't my problem. They were there to chase away the cripples, the miserable poor, the children's coffins, and to bend to the fortunate, the able-bodied. The receptionists neither. Now that I had the appropriate look, the appearance of a successful man, I was certain those pretentious old bags would regard me differently, with the highest esteem. My hypocritical flattery would be clearly welcome and appreciated. If I wanted a coffee, tons of cellulite and stretch-marks for an orgy, or whatever else, it would be all right. At your service, Monsieur! Whatever you'd like, Monsieur! My words would become currency. Folks would want to put me one a pedestal. To kiss my shoes without asking themselves if this classy fellow is who he seems to be. My problem was this: once I made it up there into the boss' office, I didn't know which language I would speak to him in. Like the vast majority of Haitians, I speak Kreyòl. And, those who speak Kreyòl have limits, we're not accorded any sort of grandeur or relevance, we're not considered gentlemen. Contrary to those who awkwardly slap two or three words in French together to show off, earning their place and that of others. There was one final problem: how would I administer the poison?

Above all, I had to be clever.

FORTY-ONE

I had pretty much perfected my plan: not to shake hands. Straighten your shoulders. Speak with calm and simple gestures, adopt a mysterious air and a low voice. Never lower your gaze. Force the other person to lose their grip. Destabilize them. And seize that moment to finish the job.

The delivery man was well disguised in his suit. You would've thought that he wasn't there, that he never existed. P had become another person, a real monster.

I don't know how people manage to live their lives in a suit, precious and captive to their eternal desire of good looks. Goddamn! I was burning up and sticky all over, plus I had to act natural, like a fish in water!

I slipped a tiny flask of poison into the inside pocket of my jacket—here we go! I asked the taxi driver to drop me off a couple blocks away from the newspaper. That way, nobody would notice my arrival. Before I got out, I checked all my equipment for the nth time. My watch. My glasses. I recalled that wealthy people always have a watch and reading glasses, so I added them to my shopping list. My shoes. My tie. I patted my heart. Everything was perfect and in place. It's true, I was well dressed, but the important question remained: Did my face match my clothes? Putting on a nice suit to look important, is that all it takes for a miserable, louse of a delivery man to make a good impression? Is it worth it to go this far? Isn't the Other Within the schizophrenic voice of death pestering me to go home? Once more, my sense of assurance was out the window. I was panicking. My legs gave out. Like a runner at the starting line hoping they never fire the shot.

The two morons stepped aside to let me through, each bowing their head respectfully, 'Well, hello monsieur!' Ordinarily, the powerful, the truly powerful don't respond, so I zipped it. I quickened my pace. At the reception desk, behind the receptionists, was an imposing portrait of the boss on this year's calendar, holding various editions of the newspaper. 'Well, hello monsieur!' they too said, smiling, wearing a white blouse with light blue jeans, less ugly that way.

This time, I answered with a tone of contempt, 'The director, quickly please!'

'Yes, of course, monsieur! We'll let you up, do you know where the director's office is located?'

'Yes,' I lied.

Climbing the stairs (I felt as if I had done this in another life), the Other Within whispered softly, as though no one else should know what he'd just decided, 'We've just found our road to Damascus, we're a team from now on, we'll get rid of all the assholes in this city.' From now on, his wishes were mine, one and the same, I was his physical presence, his true form. I remembered what he'd told me the night before, as though it were an answer to the many questions I'd asked myself about him all along: 'I'm not just some voice inside your head, some version of yourself, but the submerged, realistic, determined part of yourself that takes control of things, that stands tall when you falter. I'm the child abandoned on the side of the road, all the memories whose control you've been trying to escape, a long pent-up anger.'

I thought about the lakou, the Very Old Sheep, the day he died, the highest branch of the baobab had fallen. I thought about the girl who disappeared, about the astonishing dexterity with which she massaged my feet—you're still so tense, this'll help put your mind at ease—I recalled the sadness deep in her eyes. What kind of abyss must she have found herself in while, at this very moment, I was preparing myself to commit the irreparable?

FORTY-TWO

Needless to say, the boss was expecting someone, and the person who showed up wasn't the right one. His simultaneously anxious and confused mug said it all.

'Who are you, Monsieur? What brings you here? Do you have an appointment?'

He didn't recognize me. I felt at ease, reassured, my legs bucked back up. My plan was on track, perfect.

'Why not?'

'What do you mean, why not?'

We have the appointments we want. You think you're slick, don't you, Monsieur le Directeur, but some are cleverer than you.

'Listen, Monsieur, I don't know who you are, and you still allowed yourself to . . .'

'I'm her brother.'

'Whose brother?'

'The woman whose newspaper delivery you've been prioritizing, we've been looking for her for over a month . . .'

'I don't know what you're talking about, and what the fuck do I care?'

'You'll know soon enough.'

'All right, I'm calling the police . . .'

'I'll call your wife, then? I know one of your children (this lie wasn't necessary), would you like for me to call them, too? Maybe that way we can explain everything to one another, hmmm? What do you say, Monsieur le Directeur?'

He contemplated me with an intense, heavy stare, then he invited me to take a seat. I sat down (which wasn't too smart either, you should stand and face your adversary), adjusted my tie and cleared my throat unnecessarily after having put my briefcase down, not on the ground next to me, but right on top of his desk, an instrumental gesture I used to regain my authority.

'There's only one side to the truth,' I said, 'and secrets are like a ticking timebomb.' Apparently, you abuse the two quite a bit.

'And who's going to stand in my way? You, perhaps, Monsieur . . . What did you say your name was again?'

'I haven't told you my name, but you can call me P.'

'Do you know who I am, Monsieur P.?'

'I know enough to bury you and your newspaper in a pile of shit.'

I noticed his lips forming a shape on his face, not a smile, but a grimace of utter disgust. For half a second, I imagined him jumping out of his trap, grabbing me by the throat, trying to strangle me. His office was a bunker. Nobody came or left.

Nobody on the outside would've heard our thunderous brawl, things flying to pieces, his computer, his telephone, documents on his desk, the bookshelves, the impressive quantity of diplomas and honorary plaques on the walls, family photos. There was a kitchenette, plates, glasses, a microwave, a fruit basket, a liquor cabinet, and so on. Everything would take flight, launched by our fury.

'Drag me and my newspaper down!'

At this very moment, the expression on his face, made me think of you as you tried to hide your discomfort upon your brother's unexpected return, a good dose of hostility blended with contempt, it reminded me that I couldn't allow my plan to fail.

'Did you kill my sister, Monsieur le Directeur?'

'What!?'

'You heard me, did you kill her?'

'She didn't have a brother, she lived alone . . .'

It was impossible for the boss to be blameless.

'Now things are starting to get interesting,' I said, 'A minute ago, you didn't know what I was talking about, and now, all of a sudden, not only did you know that she lived alone, meaning you knew her, but you're also talking about her in the past tense. Don't you find that odd, Monsieur le Directeur? I'll ask again, where is my sister? How many other women have you disappeared? Are you an old, perverted psychopath? Answer my questions!'

His face revealed a mixture of irritation and fear. His upper lip trembled. His eyelashes fluttered with irregularity. He wouldn't hold back much longer.

'I don't fucking believe it!' he shouted as he pounded his fist on the desk, 'You're really pissing me off right now!'

'Are you done?'

'Yes, I'm done! Why don't you go see the so-called leaders of this country who put everything where it doesn't belong, just so they can continue robbing a corpse. I run a newspaper. I put people back to work, and I do everything I can to keep it going. You have no idea what it's like, running a business in a climate like this, taking risks, rebuilding, especially after such a devastating earthquake . . .'

'That's not what we're talking about, Monsieur le Directeur.'

'Since it's not what we're talking about . . .' He clenched his jaw, grabbed a pen and then his fat cheque book. 'Tell me, what's your price?'

'What's my price? Two coffees,' I said without hesitation.

Ha ha ha! I'll never forget the face he made, a huge ball of confusion.

'Wha . . . what did you say?'

'Two coffees, that's my price.'

'OK, fine, I've heard enough, now get the fuck out of here . . . Go!'

At this point, it's important to note that how uncanny an experience this was for me. From the moment I slipped into this suit, my true face began to fade, heeding space to this gentlemanly buffoon, like an equinox, until this very minute where the boss appeared to be completely overcome by the turn our conversation had taken. The suit had bestowed upon me such freedom and power that it was hardly believable. But how do you harness the power of your own metamorphosis, your own escape, to surpass your inner limits, to exist alongside yourself, to watch yourself play, to extend yourself into another? The well-dressed man and me, the poor, insignificant delivery man, we incarnated two appearances, two voices, fighting so that justice could be served for the same victim. I'd say it was fundamental, essential that we remain split in two, certainly, but soldered together in the accomplishment of this act. Each one respected his role, whether being (neither) entirely himself, (nor) entirely the other, without an ounce of duplicity, without experiencing the loss of his own scenic existence, or the opposite. Such a shift would have been catastrophic. Imagine if the boss, in a moment of lucidity, shouted, 'Fuck, it's you! You're my delivery man! What the fuck are you doing in my office in this get-up and who the fuck are you talking to like that?'

'I said, get out of my office!'

The more the boss lost his footing, the easier he made things for me, the more I had confidence in myself, and I found the words I needed.

'Listen, Monsieur le Directeur, I'm sure that you wouldn't want me to leave with this business left unresolved. You're a father and a business leader. Your reputation is precious to you. Your name can't get caught up in a story like this. Imagine the buzz it'll cause when everyone learns that the director of the country's premiere daily newspaper is an old pervert, a psychopath, a kidnapper, a murderer of women. And once you've fallen into disgrace, you'll lose all your credibility, you'll lose your wife, your children, your mistresses, your associates, your subscribers. Nobody will trust you any more. From now on, you'll be an assassin in everyone's eyes. Understand this, I'm as much your saviour as I am your gravedigger. Would you like to buy my trust, why not? But, if you do, give me what I'm asking for: two coffees. One for you, one for me. Are you ready to witness your life going up in flames for refusing to have coffee with a stranger?'

My lies, despite his reluctance to believe me, seemed more or less factual. He went to press a button on his office phone, undoubtedly, to ask for someone to bring us two coffees, but I stopped him. 'I want you to brew the coffee, Monsieur le Directeur.'

'Go fuck yourself!' he shouted, 'Motherfucker, who do you think you are?'

I kept my cool.

'It's your call, Monsieur le Directeur.'

He stared at me cruelly, then stood up, 'I'll make you a coffee, after that, you'll get the fuck out of here, and I won't hear about you again!'

'You have my word, Monsieur le Directeur.'

Knock knock knock! Someone was knocking at the door. 'Go away!' he shouted from the kitchenette where he was boiling water in a kettle. Then, he poured the water into a coffee press that he'd already loaded with two scoops of grounds. Stirred it with a wooden spatula. Inserted a filter. Waited, for about two minutes, before pressing the coffee. During this time, my hand discreetly slid the flask containing the poison out of the inner pocket of my coat. The big oaf was going to serve me, but this charade had gone on long enough, so I grabbed a hold of the cups, 'Allow me, Monsieur le Directeur.'

Anxious to see me disappear from his office, he emptied his poisoned cup in one gulp, and was immediately seized by violent convulsions. He choked, emitting a strange noise like an animal caught in the grips of hell. His bloodshot eyes poured a stream of tears, a mixture of blood and coffee flowed from his mouth. 'What the fuck did you do to me,' he growled, bent over and completely fucked, the bastard. The old man from Rue Magasin-de-l'État was an honest man. He swore, 'On my life and the life of my kids.' No living soul could withstand this poison. The newspaper's strongman was still writhing horribly, expiring right in front my eyes while I smiled, with a majestic sense of pride. 'Apparently coffee doesn't sit well with you, my dear boss,' I said.

In hearing this, his eyes opened wide, surprised and furious, he'd just recognized the sad delivery man and realized he was trapped.

In a last-ditch effort, I don't know exactly how, my boss leapt at me and dragged me to the floor with all his weight. A horrendous melee ensued. But he weakened very quickly, the poison was ruining his insides. I took control and finished him off with shots to the head. At least twenty at first, but then I didn't stop, I imagined seeing the Emperor's face instead of his, a face bathed in my Enlightened Colleague's tears, a face that resembled the child on the side of the road, a face that resembled all the misery of the world. I grabbed his neck with both hands and closed them with all my might . . .

I picked up my briefcase and left.

Knock knock knock!